The Thinking-About-Gladys Machine

The Thinking-About-Gladys Machine

Mario Levrero

Translated from the Spanish by
Annie McDermott and Kit Schluter

SHEFFIELD – LONDON – NEW YORK

First published in English in 2024 by And Other Stories
Sheffield – London – New York
www.andotherstories.org

1 3 5 7 9 8 6 4 2

ISBN: 9781916751064
eBook ISBN: 9781916751071

Typesetter: Tetragon, London; Typefaces: Albertan Pro and Linotype
Syntax (interior) and Stellage (cover); Series Cover Design: Elisa
von Randow, Alles Blau Studio, Brazil, after a concept by And
Other Stories; Author Photo: Eduardo Abel Giménez

And Other Stories books are printed and bound in the UK on FSC-
certified paper by the CPI Group (UK) Ltd, Croydon. The covers are of
299gsm Vanguard card, containing a minimum of 30% upcycled fibre,
and are made in the Lake District at the environmentally friendly James
Cropper paper mill. They are embossed with biodegradable foils.

A catalogue record for this book is available from the British Library.

And Other Stories gratefully acknowledge that our work is supported using
public funding by Arts Council England and that the translation of this
book was partially funded by the support of a grant from English PEN's PEN
Translates programme, which is supported by Arts Council England.

Supported using public funding by
**ARTS COUNCIL
ENGLAND**

FREEDOM
TO **WRITE**
FREEDOM
TO **READ**

MIX
Paper | Supporting
responsible forestry
FSC® C171272

CONTENTS

THE BOOK AND THE TEXTS

(NOTE ON THE 1995 EDITION)

For almost twenty-five years now, *The Thinking-About-Gladys Machine* has been practically non-existent. It was published in December 1970, just a few days after *La Ciudad* (*The City*), a novel that earned a mention in the weekly newspaper *Marcha*, and which, perhaps as a result, fared a bit better. *Gladys*, meanwhile, hardly made it into bookshops; according to some booksellers, the distributor's reps said they hadn't even heard of it. I never found out if a decision had been made not to promote it, or if it was just a general lack of interest from both the publishers and the reading public. It was a time of 'topical issues', and the books that were attracting attention tended to have very definite sources of inspiration. The really surprising thing, then, is that I managed to publish these books at all. The credit, or the blame, is due to one Marcial Souto, who worked hard to set up, within an 'ideologically committed' publishing house, a series called Literatura Diferente, which gave a home to works by José Pedro Díaz, Carlos Casacuberta, Dean Koontz and Robert Sheckley, among others.

Some of the pieces that make up this book were previously published in magazines and supplements (*Señal*, the *El Popular* newspaper's *Revista de los Viernes, Maldoror, El Lagrimal Trifurca*), and the novella *Jelly* appeared in a chapbook insert of the magazine *Los Huevos del Plata*. After the book came out, and then vanished, the stories went on to be published elsewhere, some of them many times, in magazines, newspapers and anthologies from various countries.

Meanwhile, the publishing house Tierra Nueva had moved from Uruguay to Argentina, and for some reason thought to take along the copies of *Gladys* they had in storage. Several friends spotted the book on the sale tables of the bookshops on Calle Corrientes in Buenos Aires, and that's how more Argentines than Uruguayans came to have copies in their possession. Later on, it's said, the remaining copies – that is, almost the entire print run – were turned back into pulp, and that very paper pulp might just be supporting a worthy book today.

Allow me, then, to dedicate this second edition of *The Thinking-About-Gladys Machine* to everyone who looked for the first one, whether or not they found it in the end. For all those years, it meant a lot to know that people were out there looking for it.

ML, *February 1995*
Tr. *KS*

THE THINKING-ABOUT-GLADYS MACHINE

Before going to bed I made my daily rounds of the house, to check everything was in order; the window was open in the small bathroom at the back, so the polyester shirt I was going to wear the next day could dry overnight; I shut the door (to prevent draughts); in the kitchen, the tap was dripping and I tightened it; the window was open and I left it that way – though I did close the blind – and the rubbish had been taken out; the three knobs on the stove were all at zero; the dial on the fridge was at three (light refrigeration) and the half-drunk bottle of mineral water was sealed with its plastic cap; in the dining room, the big clock wouldn't need winding for several more days and the table had been cleared; in the library I had to turn off the amp, which someone had left on, but the turntable had switched itself off automatically; the ashtray on the armchair had been emptied, the thinking-about-Gladys machine was plugged in and purring away softly as usual, and the high little window that looks onto the air shaft was open, with the smoke from the day's cigarettes slowly drifting through it; I shut the door; in the living room I found a cigarette butt on the floor and placed it in the standing ashtray, which it's the maid's job to empty every morning; in my bedroom I wound the alarm clock, making sure it was showing the same time as my wristwatch, and set it to go off half an hour later the next morning (because I'd decided to skip my shower; I could feel a cold coming on); I lay down and turned out the light.

In the early hours I woke up feeling anxious; an unusual noise had made me jump; I curled up in bed with all the pillows on top of me and clutched the back of my neck and waited tensely for the end: the house was falling down.

Tr. AM

BEGGAR STREET

I take out a cigarette and put it to my lips, but when I bring the lighter close and spin the wheel, it won't light. I'm surprised, because it was working perfectly just a few moments ago, with a strong flame, and there wasn't any sign the fuel was running low; what's more, I remember replacing the flint and refilling it only a couple of hours ago.

Over and over, I flick the wheel without success; I make sure it's producing a spark, and then refill the tank with an eye-dropper.

Still, it won't light.

It hasn't failed like this for years. I decide to locate the defect.

Once again, I use a coin to take out the screw that keeps the tank shut; this doesn't seem to help dismantle it. With the same coin, I go on to remove the screw from the flint tube; a spring pops out as well, propped on the end of the screw. On the other end of the spring, there's a piece of metal resembling the flint (which also comes out, along with a few white filaments the same length as the spring, which

I'd never noticed before). The lighter is still in one piece; removing those screws hasn't got me anywhere.

Looking more closely, I notice a third screw: the one that serves as an axle for the lever that turns the wheel and produces the spark. I decide to take it out as well, but the coin is no help; I have to use a small screwdriver instead.

I have a whole collection of screwdrivers. There are plenty of them, organised by size, and each proportionate to the next. I use the smallest – though I could have achieved the same result with the no. 2 or the no. 3.

Several parts come out now: the lever, the screw in question (with a nut on its other end, though from the outside this nut looks just like a screw; the hidden part is hollow), two or three springs and the little serrated wheel, which rolls merrily over the table, falls to the floor, and now I can't find it anywhere.

Even so, the lighter still looks whole to me; there's something aggressive about its solidity – a kind of challenge. And the defect remains a mystery. I stick the screwdriver into various holes; first, it goes all the way through the flint tube, and pokes out of the top; I find some cotton wool in the tank, and explore no further; then I inspect the holes in the upper section of the lighter. There are two: one is the end of another tube, whose function I am unaware of; this tube has a bend in it, which the screwdriver can't get past. The other tube is wider, and straight; at the end of it – at a distance I estimate to be about half the length of the lighter – the tool stops suddenly mid-spin, caught on the head of a screw, which I decide to remove; it's short and wide. Then I pull on a small protruding part with my fingertips, while holding the outer shell of the lighter with my left hand. Much to my satisfaction, I see something sliding out.

The thin metal case is still in my left hand. When the inner section emerges, the metal contraption suddenly expands with a click (and I'm surprised to see it grow around four times larger). My right hand is now holding a giant replica of the lighter, which more or less retains its proportions and general appearance, though with a great many new nooks and crannies. I imagine the system of springs I'm going to have to squeeze back together in order to return this contraption to its casing (and I have no idea how I'm going to manage it, though I suspect it won't be easy); only springs could explain such startling growth.

By poking the screwdriver into a number of holes, I discover some unexpected screws, but by now the no. 1 is too small for them. It doesn't apply an even force and I'm worried they might get stripped. I choose another; the no. 4 is ideal, though I could just as well use the no. 3 or the no. 5, maybe the no. 6, or even the no. 7.

I remove several screws. More springs fall out, and a single oiled metal piece (resembling a piston) drops out of a tube, along with a couple of cogs.

I discover that this contraption is also made up of two parts, an outer and an inner; when I can't find any more screws, I go ahead and pull them apart, following the same process as before. The whole phenomenon repeats right on cue, and I find myself holding a structure some four times larger than the last (and sixteen times larger than the lighter itself), though still of more or less the same weight. I'd even say this structure weighs less than the whole lighter, which may seem strange at first – especially when you're holding it in the palm of your hand – but the logic stands. By law, the contents must weigh less than the lighter as a whole, even if they've increased in size by means of that ingenious spring mechanism and so appear heavier.

I decide to take out the cotton wool; it seems extremely tightly packed (which explains how the fluid can last for so many days inside the tank – much longer than in other lighters). The tank has grown proportionally, and now the cotton wool is looser; all in all, there must be several large bags' worth in there. Removing it doesn't require much effort, because my whole hand can fit inside the tank now.

By this point, I can tell it's going to be very difficult indeed to put the lighter back together; I may not be able to use it again. But that doesn't matter; my curiosity about the mechanism drives me on. I'm no longer interested in finding the cause of the problem (and I doubt I'm in any state even to notice where that problem is), but rather in getting a general sense of the structure of certain lighters.

I'm not using a screwdriver to explore the tubes any more; my hand can now fit comfortably inside most of them. Some have a curious, almost labyrinthine intricacy; my hand sometimes lands on several openings along the same tube, and begins feeling around inside one, only to find that it's the beginning, or end, of another, which itself contains several openings to various other tubes. There aren't as many screws now, and there seem to be fewer springs at play.

Following one of the pipes and some of its offshoots with my hand and part of my arm, I reach a place that seems to be near the structure's centre. There, my fingers land on a number of little metal balls. They have the peculiarity of being half-exposed, like the tips of ballpoint pens; I can make them spin by rolling my finger over them.

I press down harder on one and it pops loose from the metal plate holding it in place. It starts rolling along the tubes, and drops out of the structure. I notice it's the same size as one of those marbles kids play with. Lots come tumbling out after it. Ten or twelve – maybe more. I pick one up and its weight surprises me; it seems as heavy as the rest of the structure. But if it were, then I wouldn't be able to explain how it fitted inside the lighter in the first place. I expect these balls also expanded by means of a system of springs. Their weight continues to intrigue me.

All of a sudden, I feel sleep coming on. I look at my watch and see that it's two in the morning. It's amazing how you can lose track of time when you're distracted by something interesting. I think I ought to go to bed, but I can't give up on my project. I'll keep going, I decide, until I reach the final structure, or until the lighter is completely dismantled, broken down into each of its constituent parts.

Now, after a couple more operations, by means of which I separate the structure into two parts again (one layer, or shell, and one quadruple-sized structure), the lighter takes up more than half the room. This latest structure doesn't resemble the original lighter at all; its forms are less rigid, there are curves. If the space allowed me to look at it from a distance, I might find it's almost spherical.

My only route from one side of the room to the other is now through the lighter. I can make it across fairly easily, though I do need to crawl. It strikes me that if I were to separate it into two again, I'd end up with a structure I could walk around in standing up. But I fear, indeed I'm almost certain, that it would no longer fit inside the room.

So far I've only used one of the tubes, which runs in a straight line from one side of the lighter to the other; but there are more, and I'm tempted to explore them as well. Labyrinths terrify me, so I take a spool of thread, tie one end to a handle on the chest of drawers, and make my way into a tube, which quickly changes direction and leads me to others.

They're soft, despite being made of metal. Or, rather than 'soft', I should say they're 'springy'; the spring action is still tangible. I swear aloud at myself: I didn't think to bring a flashlight or even a box of matches. I work my hand laboriously into my pocket, and then burst out laughing. I'd instinctively reached for my lighter, forgetting that I was inside it.

'I have to go back for the flashlight,' I think, and just as I'm getting ready to follow the thread out, I see a faint light ahead. 'An exit, or maybe the same hole I came in by,' I wonder, and keep on crawling towards the light, which grows brighter and brighter.

By now, I'm able to make out some of my surroundings. The place isn't exactly a tunnel, in the sense of a closed, tubular channel. Rather, it's made up of countless tiny sections, though there are large metal beams running through it, some wider than my body; I can't tell where they begin or end.

I keep going, without reaching the outside. The light has grown more intense – which is to say, it's a little brighter than a candle. I still can't work out where it's coming from.

At this point, I find I'm able to stand up and walk – though hunching over slightly.

I hear moans.

'This is the street of the beggars,' I think to myself, turning the corner, and then I see the light source – a street-lamp – and overhead, the stars.

And sure enough, there are beggars asking for change, with ulcers all over their arms and legs. The street is cobbled and sloping. The shops are closed, the shutters down.

'I've got to find a bar that's open,' I think. 'I need cigarettes, and matches.'

August 1967
Tr. KS

ONE-WAY STORY NO. 2

A dog, Champion. I lived alone with him and he started getting on my nerves. I walked him out to the woods, left him tied up with some rope he could break without too much persistence, and went back home.

A couple of days later I found him pawing at the door; I let him in.

That's when he became completely unbearable. I took him out to a more distant wood and tied him to a tree with thicker rope (I knew the problem didn't lie in the rope, but in the animal's loyalty; maybe I secretly hoped he wouldn't be able to break free this time and would die of hunger).

He came back again in a few days.

I realised then that the dog would always come back. I didn't dare kill him for fear of regret; even if I did manage to lose him, I thought, in some even more distant wood, I would live in constant fear of his return; it would torment my nights and spoil all my happy moments. I'd be tied up more by his absence than by his presence.

I hesitated for just a moment, faced with the majesty of the dense forest that stood before my eyes – gloomy, imposing, mysterious. Then, resolutely, I started walking in, and kept walking until, finally, I was lost.

Tr. KS

THE ABANDONED HOUSE

LOCATION

On a central street where most of the buildings are modern, there is, however, one old abandoned house. In front is a garden, separated from the pavement by a fence, and in the garden a bright white fountain, adorned with little angels. The fence looks like a row of rusty spears, joined together by two horizontal bars. As for the house, all you can see from outside is the once pink, now dirty-green colour of the façade, and part of a very dark blind.

This house only interests the select few people who fall under its influence. These people, among whom I count myself, know about certain things that happen there.

LITTLE MEN

An inch of pipe can be seen protruding from the wall in one room, which most likely formed part of the gas system.

If you're lucky, or patient, you'll spot the tiny men, four or so inches tall, who poke their heads out and gaze around, as if seeing the ocean for the first time through a porthole. They then try to extricate themselves, which is no easy task; to begin with, they have to lie on their backs and grip the top edge of the pipe, and then, with the help of their arm muscles, and also their legs, they gradually work their bodies free.

They hang in the air, swaying gently.

The little man glances down and gets a fright, because instead of the floor there's an enormous hole (these activities have clearly, over time, made the battered wooden boards give way). Meanwhile, inside the pipe, you can see the round, gleaming eyes of the next little man, impatiently waiting his turn.

They hold out as long as they can, but eventually they take a deep breath, as if before a dive, then their hands let go of the edge of the pipe and the little men fall and fall.

Because you're expecting it, you might – after a second – think you hear something, but those familiar with the spectacle know there's no sound. Some people imagine a muffled plop, like the bounce of a rubber ball; others a sharp, skeletal crack. The more inventive describe a small explosion (like stepping on a match, they say, but without the ensuing blaze), and similarly, there are those who speak of implosion, because they're reminded of an electric light blowing (as distinct from the shattering of the bulb).

Others even swear they can clearly make out the sound of breaking glass.

We've been down to the basement, but its perimeter doesn't quite seem to match the shape of the house. Nor are there any holes in the ceiling that might correspond to the one in the floor above, through which the little men vanish.

We suspect there are tiny corpses piling up somewhere in the house; we feel uneasy because we can't find them.

My own, admittedly baseless theory, which I air in casual conversations, is that the little men don't die when they fall, and that, what's more, they are few in number and eternal and on an endless loop.

SPIDERS

One thing that surprised the discoverers and early fans of the house was the seemingly total lack of spiders. You could find anything and everything in there, but – contrary to expectations – no spider appeared remotely interested in that thoroughly suitable place. This mistaken impression was set right when they visited the pantry, which is next to the kitchen.

The place is full of spiders.

There's a vast array of species, shapes, sizes, colours, ages and habits, and the webs form a kind of spongy filling that takes up the whole room. If you look carefully, however, you'll find that each web maintains an appropriate distance from those of rival spiders; the most that's permitted (and this seems to be an accepted rule) is to use another spider's web as a support, or starting point, for one's own.

A great sense of peace presides over the pantry; the creatures lie in wait. Some at the centre of their webs, others lurking near the edges, others hidden from view, and still others apparently daydreaming on the walls or the ceiling. It's not the kind of wait that bystanders hope to see the end of.

Many spiders – generally the largest – don't have webs, and instead occupy a kind of nest on the floor; those ones aren't often seen. They mostly come out of their nest on very hot days, or particular nights, or at times when we don't, quite honestly, see any reason for them to come out at all.

We think the spiders are in there because of the no doubt extremely favourable conditions. What we can't explain, however, is their stubborn refusal to occupy other parts of the house. We've seen some linger in the doorway but never actually leave; and we've seen others leave, only to scuttle hastily back, as if drawn by an irresistible force or impelled by a kind of terror.

When at rest, the arrangement of webs is itself a beautiful, ever-changing spectacle, enhanced by the equally changeable light that filters in, through a little window, as the day wears on and dies. The damp air also plays a role, as do the observer's mood and several unfathomable factors.

An insect lands in one of the countless traps: everything vibrates. (Now and then we bring some flies in a jar and set things in motion ourselves, but more often we like to leave it to chance.) First there's a slight, barely perceptible tremor, caused by the insect hitting the web, and this then spreads from the web to the rest of the system. The insect, needless to say, grows ever more distressed, and struggles ever harder to break free. The system moves in sympathy, undulating to the same rhythm, forming ripples that rebound and overlap – as if you could see the effect of throwing pebbles into the ocean in three, rather than two, dimensions.

And then the spiders spring into action: first the owner of the web that caught the insect, who, watched closely by her neighbour, hurries towards her victim and gets down to business. Her swift, dainty movement across the web, and the work that follows, together create a different, more pronounced effect, and then all the nearby spiders, who have felt their webs shake yet not located the victim, begin darting all over, searching high and low, peering at other spiders' webs and then back at their own, and perhaps losing their temper when they don't find anything there.

Now the performance reaches its fullest splendour; now we sink, enraptured, into a kind of trance. Some people have even been known to dance (because there is a rhythm, which grows increasingly frenetic); others cover their eyes because they can't bear it.

I myself once had to restrain someone who, as if he'd been hypnotised, tried to plunge into the room (I heard that some time later he drowned himself, at night, in the sea).

The spiders, as I've said, have trouble leaving that room, and never do so for very long or stray very far. There are, however, exceptions.

PICNICS

We discovered by chance that, beneath the pink wallpaper in the bedroom, there was some paper of a different kind. A team formed right away – headed up by Ramírez – and after a few nights of intensive, painstaking work they managed to remove all the pink and reveal what had been there before, which mostly involved shades of green.

It showed a beautiful rural landscape, and was impressively realistic: we could almost taste the fresh, invigorating country air. The damaged sections were masterfully restored by Alfredo (a quiet guy with a moustache, who we never suspected of having any skills).

Inspired by the newly uncovered wallpaper, we felt we ought to organise a series of Sunday picnics. We got up early and gathered with baskets and folding chairs; Juancito, who worked in a corner shop, brought along a cooler of Coca-Cola; we also had red wine, a battery-powered record player, children with butterfly nets, butterflies (provided by an entomologist friend, on the condition they were returned unharmed), brightly coloured dresses, young couples, ants, the odd small spider (which we brought from the pantry), and other things besides.

The main attraction was a device invented by Chueco, who worked on building sites in his spare time: a barbecue that ran on cooking gas, and had some mechanism for getting rid of the smoke. And, although it served no practical purpose, the tree Alfredo made from some synthetic fibre also went down very well.

I used to sit on the floor in a corner and drink maté. Picnics aren't my thing, but the sight of these ones warmed my heart.

IT

Something pulsates, something grows in the attic.

We suspect that it's green, we fear it has eyes.

We imagine it's strong, squishy, translucent, malign.

We must not, will not, cannot see it.

To speak of it we use only adjectives, and avoid each other's gaze.

We don't go up the creaking staircase; we don't stand on the threshold to listen; we don't reach out and turn the handle; we don't open the attic door.

LITTLE WOMEN

To see the little men who emerge from the gas pipe you have to wait and wait. Meanwhile, you need only fill the bathroom sink with lukewarm water and turn on the tap, and within a minute the little women will come pouring out. They're very small and they're naked. Our presence doesn't make them self-conscious; on the contrary, they swim around freely, splash in the water, clamber onto a plastic soap dish we put there especially and stretch out as if in the sun. They are beautiful without exception; their bodies are splendid and exciting; they dive in and swim underwater, and splash on the surface, and clamber back onto the soap dish and stretch out once more as if in the sun.

When the time comes, between them they pull out the plug and let the water wash them away.

(There's one with green eyes who's the last to go. She looks at me with a kind of pity before sliding down the drain.)

AN EXCEPTION

One afternoon, Ramírez — an accountant in a fairly major factory — was on his way home, after investigating, along with the rest of us, the many-layered wallpaper in the master bedroom of the abandoned house (he was the one who analysed layer number five, deducing the whole scene – correctly, we later confirmed – based on three visible square inches; for obvious reasons – I must remind the reader that there are ladies in our group – he didn't go into detail, but he said it was an erotic, practically pornographic scene, thus giving rise to our theory that the house once served as a brothel). A very old lady ran after him for quite some way, eventually catching him up and explaining, so breathless and flustered that she could barely get the words out, that behind him, on his jacket, near his neck, there was a very black spider almost three inches in diameter.

Whenever we phoned to invite him to the abandoned house, Ramírez would make excuses. In the end, he told us the story and we understood.

He says that when the old lady finally got her point across, he didn't have the wherewithal to remove his jacket. Instead, he escaped from within it, and the jacket hung in the air for a moment, emptied of its wearer. Ramírez says he was half a block away before he heard his jacket hit the ground with a thud.

COLLAPSE

I feel very drawn to the house's serene, tireless collapse. I measure the cracks and record their progress, along with the dark edges of the spreading damp, the chunks of plaster that come loose from the walls and ceiling, and the way

THE ENTIRE THING TILTS, barely perceptibly, leftwards; an inevitable, beautiful collapse.

THE GARDEN

We can't come to an agreement about the area of the garden. We all accept that, seen from the fence, or from the path that divides it in two and leads to the house, it looks to be about eighty square yards (8 × 10). The arguments begin, however, when one of us ventures in among its bushes, its fronds of ivy, its flowerless plants, the insects, the ant trails, the vines and giant ferns, the rays of sunlight that filter, here and there, through the leaves of the tall eucalyptus trees; the bear prints, the chatter of parakeets, the snakes – coiled around branches – who raise their heads and hiss when we get too close, and the unbearable heat, the thirst, the darkness, the roaring of leopards, the blows of the machete as we hack our way through, the high boots, the humidity, the helmets, the lush vegetation, the night, the fear, the not finding a way out, never finding a way out.

THE SEARCH

Almost none of us can let go of the idea that the house contains an ancient, fabulous treasure, made up of precious stones and thick, heavy gold coins. There are no maps or references of any kind to support this idea. I count myself among the sceptics, though I admit I often give in to temptation and dream, and even find myself imagining sneaky unexpected nooks and crannies where the treasure might be hidden. What sets me apart from the others is the fact I don't look for it, either alone (as I know many people do) or during the official searches.

I find these searches most enjoyable. I settle in a recliner that I bring from home especially and position in a suitable spot, generally the middle room. And then, while sipping maté and smoking cigarettes, I watch as everyone spreads out methodically – the ladies taking the house, the men the basement – to search. The ladies, in their jolly dresses, rummage through the debris or inside the upholstery (and I smile when I see them looking in items of furniture that they know full well we brought here ourselves as fuel for the hurricanes). The men, in blue uniforms, knock on the walls of the basement, listening for a hollow or different sound; but every sound is hollow, and different from the last, and this gives rise to a kind of music that reminds me of hitting bottles filled with varying amounts of liquid. After a while it all seems to come together and the music takes on a powerful rhythm and the women search high and low as if they're dancing and I think once again of musical bottles, now containing liqueurs, all different colours, all transparent and sweet.

Of course it was a woman, Leonor – that finicky spinster who latched on to our group, though I have no idea why (she's afraid of the house) – who turned on the bidet tap. Everyone knows that the running water has been cut off, that it's dangerous to go around turning on taps with no warning, that little women come out of the tap in the sink, that the tap in the bath produces a rubbery, yellowish thing which inflates like a balloon and doesn't stop inflating until you turn the tap off (at which point it detaches and hovers in our midst for a while, before floating up and sticking to the ceiling, where it stays until one day we go in and it's no longer there); and that when we flush the toilet, by the old-fashioned means of pulling a chain with a wooden handle on the end, we hear that dreadful, interminable howl that gives us goosebumps and makes us worry what the neighbours will say.

We heard a scream that we mistook for that very howl, but no, it was Leonor, who came running in, pointing at the bathroom, and when we went to investigate we saw a thin black worm emerging from one of the little holes in the bidet, and emerging some more, and by then it was easily four feet long. We waited to see if it would stop, but it went on coming out and slithering over the floor, now aiming for other rooms.

We cut it into bits and each one remained completely alive, wriggling out of our reach. We had to sweep them up and push them through the grate, but the thing was still coming out and soon new heads began appearing in the other holes. We tried to turn off the tap but it was jammed, and no one felt like changing the washer, let alone calling a plumber, and just as we were thinking there was nothing for it but to declare the bathroom out of bounds as well and lose sight of the little women forever (Leonor was accused of having done it on purpose), someone had the presence of mind (and the courage) to try directing the heads down the plughole of the bidet itself. The worms seemed quite happy with this, because they went on slithering out and back in again, and so it goes on, that continuous, apparently endless thing. Anyone who encounters the bidet without knowing the story will think they're looking at a strange, horizontal shower of glistening black rain.

HURRICANE

A flutter of ash and cigarette ends in the wood stove in the dining room; then it's best to get out, or shut yourself in the bedroom, or, as a last resort, stay put, huddled in a corner, your head between your knees and your hands covering your head.

Dirt, papers, random objects, all begin swirling gently – like fallen leaves – in the middle of the room. The temperature drops abruptly and the wind blows harder and harder, and now everything's spinning, drawn towards the centre, and the furniture is dragged along and the walls shake, and then the plaster starts to crumble, and the dust chokes us and gets in our eyes and makes us thirsty. Anyone caught unawares is trapped, and ends up spinning and spinning. From time to time they're hurled against a wall, bounce off it and return to the centre, and so it goes on until they die and perhaps even after they die.

When calm returns, I leave the corner and stroll through the rubble, the broken vases, the overturned furniture. Everything is gloriously out of place. The living room looks tired, as if it had vomited.

And we can all, it seems, breathe a little more easily.

THE UNICORN

We think it's attracted by the herb. Of course, we can't be sure of anything, and our theories on the matter have no scientific basis. But it's worth recording some details.

We have classified the herb (a task carried out by Ángel, the vegetarian) as a native variety – apparently occurring only in this garden – of *Martynia louisiana*, which grows in North America. It has big, yellowish flowers with purple spots. Once a year it bears fruit: a seed pod with a pointed tip, shaped like a horn.

Hence its common name, 'unicorn plant', and hence – we believe – the yearly visit of that animal to our garden.

Despite patient surveillance, we still haven't seen it. We have, however, seen toothmarks on the herb. We have seen a hole in the soil – as if made by the tapered end of an umbrella – by the raised edge of a pond; we have seen hoofprints; we have found fresh manure. One night we heard a soft whinnying on the breeze, and the next morning we found Luisa – a sixteen-year-old who had joined our group just days before – with her chest pierced by a single, enormous hole, naked, monstrously raped.

YOU

You are a door-to-door salesman, flogging books or medical insurance. You knock on all the doors, try to gain access to all the houses.

It's the afternoon. You see a fence and hesitate for a moment – but you're determined, and that overgrown garden doesn't put you off. You push the gate open, walk up the path that divides the garden in two, stop at the door and look for the bell.

You don't find it, but you do find a bronze knocker. It's shaped like a hand, with long, slender fingers – a big ring on the longest – and missing, not because it's broken but because it was made that way, a couple of joints from the index finger. Your own hand, on noticing this, falters slightly, but then you remember some lessons from salesman school, and a few examples from your personal experience, and you complete the action, taking the knocker, lifting it – so that it hinges upwards – and letting it fall once, twice, three times onto its base – which is also bronze. Inside the house, the sound booms.

This confuses you; we, meanwhile, from unfortunate experience, know only too well that a knock at the door sets off a whole host of strange echoes within the house, which invariably give the impression of a dry, rasping voice insisting that you open the door and come in. Your confusion doesn't last long: you take your hopes for reality and make the fateful mistake.

When we arrive, we find your briefcase on a chair, or on the floor; we don't need to open it to know your line of work. We gather in the dining room and hold a minute's silence.

Someone always sheds a tear. Someone else always suggests reporting the case to the authorities; we convince them that it wouldn't get us anywhere and would instead lose us the house. Then someone pipes up and suggests putting a warning sign by the entrance.

We older types have to explain, once again, that this would be a sure-fire way of increasing the number of victims and that, sooner or later, the curious idiots would get us thrown out.

In the end everyone agrees that although these cases are regrettable, it's not in our power to prevent them. Finally, tired after so many sad scenes, weights on our conscience and pointless arguments, we try to see the funny side and say that there are, after all, too many door-to-door salesmen in this world.

Later on, someone takes your briefcase and throws it, quite unceremoniously, down the well behind the house.

ANTS

The garden, needless to say, is host to a variety of ants, and from time to time we're delighted to come across a new anthill; when we do, we plant a little red flag. We've noticed ants making their way along cracks to a place somewhere beneath the house, in the foundations. We think this is a factor in the building's slow collapse.

We take it upon ourselves to look after the most important plants, pruning them and giving the offcuts to the ants. The philosopher objects, on the grounds that we're contributing to the decline of the species by making their work easier, and thereby gradually reducing their capacity to do it. One lady thinks we should simply poison them with lindane – but everyone knows that's wishful thinking.

What happens inside the house is different. There are ants there too, but we never see them do any work what-soever. They're always isolated from any group, apparently deep in thought (or wandering listlessly over a wall or floor-board). We have learnt that they're few in number, that they live alone – in some crack or forgotten corner – and that they eat bits and pieces they find lying around (I've never seen them store anything). They're occasionally spotted in pairs, but these aren't lasting relationships.

There's one – we've marked her with a little white paint on her rear – who spends days on end tirelessly collecting little sticks and other small objects. She uses them all to build something that isn't a nest; we don't know what it is, and for the ant it seems to serve no practical purpose. She walks about on it, enraptured, then forgets the whole thing and returns, for a while, to her contemplative state. If, by chance or by mistake, the structure is destroyed – even partially – the ant flies into a rage and doesn't calm down for hours.

Archie, the engineer – who has carried out an exhaustive study – believes it's a giant engineering project. It would be impossible, he says, to construct something like that without an in-depth understanding of mathematics. He made a few notes, which he thinks will help him to revolutionise bridge-building techniques; in his opinion, the ant is acting instinctively and building bridges where none are needed.

I don't think they're bridges; I have my own views on the matter. Everyone uses magnifying glasses, everyone focuses on the detail and praises the meticulous work and delicately balanced little sticks. Personally, I prefer to see it as a whole and say that it's beautiful, and that its shape is not unlike that of an ant.

December 1966–January 1967
Tr. AM

THE BASEMENT

There once was a boy who lived in a very big house.

This house had a great many rooms and, although he had walked round them all (or perhaps he only thought he had), the boy didn't know it in full; his memory wasn't big enough to remember everything. And so, almost every time he went into a room, it felt like the first time, and he had no way of knowing whether he'd been in there before – though he assumed he must have been at some point.

This isn't to say that the boy sometimes got lost in his own house (or rather, his parents' house: children don't possess things, ownership being a matter for grown-ups, indeed the principal matter for grown-ups, so important that History and wars are spun on its lathe, and people simply don't leave such important things in the hands of children, who, as we all know, have a general tendency to break their toys); no, he didn't get lost in the house, and nor could he have done, seeing as the rooms were arranged on either side of long, wide hallways. There weren't many of these hallways, just four or five, and they were all very straight, and they met at the centre, where there was a fire-place and a table.

His mother would often sit at that crossing and knit, and his father would read the paper; he himself used to do his homework there, and you could say the entire life of the house revolved around that place, which they called the living room, and which, wherever they felt like going, they inevitably had to pass through.

The boy knew this place, the living room, very well, along with his bedroom, the dining room, the kitchen and the bathroom, but he never managed to understand the rest of the house in the same way.

Still, he walked around it every day, and opened every door he saw and went everywhere he wanted, and stumbled upon many things that were new to him. Sometimes he realised he'd been into a room before because he found something of his in there, something he'd lost, no doubt, on some earlier trip, such as a shirt button, the ear of a woollen dog, or a little glass marble.

Once, he came upon a locked door.

*

This seemed very strange to him, since the doors in that house were hardly ever closed, and certainly never locked. But this one had an enormous padlock on it and, despite all his efforts, it proved impossible to open because he didn't have the key.

He thought this door must lead to a room he had never been in, because he was sure he'd never seen a door with a padlock on it before, unless the padlock had only recently been put there.

This all made him very curious, and he decided to ask his parents about the meaning of that locked door. But then he got caught up in visiting other rooms, and by the time night had fallen and he was sitting down with them at the dinner table, he had forgotten all about it.

They talked about lots of different things. There were some words and phrases he didn't understand because, although he wasn't so small that he couldn't follow a normal conversation, his parents often discussed difficult subjects that lay beyond his grasp. For example: could anyone here explain the tetravalency of carbon? Or cases of irrationality in logarithms? I've never understood that kind of stuff at all myself, and that's why I'm writing stories now instead of doing something useful with my time.

But they also talked about things he understood just fine, and he talked too, recounting his experiences at school and even around the house. He described, for example, how his teacher had forgotten to put in her false teeth that day, or how he had found himself in a sumptuously decorated room with beautiful tapestries hanging on the walls, or in another that was completely empty, and his parents would listen attentively and sometimes explain things that weren't clear to him.

That night, Carlitos – which is the name of the boy in this story, I almost forgot to mention – told of how he'd been in a rather small room with a strange spinning chair in it (like the ones often found at dental clinics); there were also some glass cabinets with tongs in them and, next to the chair, a contraption of lights and pulleys – also like those seen in dental clinics.

He asked his father what all this meant, and his father replied that it was indeed a dental clinic.

*

That night he didn't ask his parents about the padlock, and the following days and nights he had other things to ask about which, though not as remarkable or surprising as the locked door, had a more immediate appeal, whether because he had laid eyes on some inexplicable, pretty-coloured object, or because questions had arisen that called for a more urgent response (like the problem his teacher set him about the spider and the fly).

His parents always seemed happy to talk to him, and never got frustrated by his questions. However, at some point in the conversation they would invariably stray from the subject down unexpected paths and go on talking among themselves about their own business, and never again during that period (lunch, dinner or the after-dinner chat) would he have a chance to make himself heard, because the subjects they touched on were so far-flung from his own, and the pauses in conversation so pregnant with thoughts or hand gestures, that he was afraid to interrupt them with his words.

But he soon stumbled upon the locked door again. It seemed to have moved to a different part of the house now, and that night he didn't forget to bring it up.

His parents, without answering directly, said they were surprised he'd never mentioned it before, seeing as that door had always been there, and had always had a padlock on it. He replied that this was only the second time he'd seen it, and the time before he'd forgotten to ask.

'Well,' said the father, 'if you forgot it once, that must mean it's not very important to you.'

'No,' the boy protested, and then he explained how amazed he'd been and gave a few reasons why he might have forgotten to ask. Then he repeated his question about the meaning behind that door.

'That door,' said his father, 'leads down to the basement.'

'And why is it locked?' Carlitos asked.

'So no one can open it,' said his mother.

'And why shouldn't anyone open it?' the boy asked again.

'So no one can go down the stairs behind it,' answered his father.

'And why shouldn't anyone go down the stairs?'

'So no one can go into the basement.'

'And why shouldn't anyone go into the basement?'

'Because there's something down there,' his father answered, 'that no one should ever know about.'

And with that, his mother and father launched into a complex and entirely unrelated discussion (something about the unified tax system) and Carlitos sat there, deep in thought, trying to work out what could be in the basement.

*

The next day, Carlitos bumped into his mother on the little gravel path that ran through the garden from the front door to the street, and asked her to let him into the basement.

'No,' she answered. 'You'll never be allowed down to the basement. You'll never find the key and you'll never, ever, *ever* be allowed in there.'

'But what's down there?' the boy persisted, with tears in his eyes.

'You'll never, ever, *ever* know,' his mother said, and then she went into the house, while the boy continued on his way to school.

At school, Carlitos couldn't stop thinking about the basement, and the day was most unpleasant because the teacher kept going on and on about toads, throughout every subject and even at break time.

Back home, the boy rushed through his homework and then set about roaming the hallways in search of the door to the basement. That day, he didn't find it.

*

The next morning, Carlitos got up earlier than usual and had the good fortune of running into the maid – a very tall, very thin (and at one point very sweet) black woman called Ermine, who, for a long time, he hadn't been able to find in any of the rooms.

As they were talking, he took the opportunity to ask about the basement. And without interrupting the delicate work she was doing with some black threads, making what looked like a giant spiderweb, she answered:

'I don't know anything about that. I don't want to know anything, either. I've never known anything. If I did, I wouldn't tell you, or I'd tell you I didn't know anything, or that I'd never known anything, or that I didn't want to know anything. I don't know anyone who knows anything, either, and I wouldn't want to know anyone who knows anything, or know anyone who's ever known or would ever like to know anything. All I know is that maybe your grandparents know something about someone who might want to know something, or who knows something, or who may once have known something.'

The woman carried on – without offering anything of deeper substance – and with each phrase she added a long, damp thread to the web, which spun endlessly around her nimble fingers. Carlitos thanked her for the information and set off to look for his grandparents.

But he hadn't seen them for a very long time, and chance

didn't help him find them. So he had to wait until the evening.

*

At dinner, he asked his father.

'Some of them are dead,' his father replied. 'Only your father's mother and your mother's father are still alive. You won't find your father's mother unless you ask your mother. However, you'll find your mother's father by walking around the house, since he's in one of the rooms. But bear in mind that you mustn't tire him out: he can only answer one question per day, and only in exchange for a peppermint sweet.'

Carlitos wanted to know more precisely where his grandfather was; he explained that it might take a long, long time to find him by chance, and that perhaps he'd never find him at all.

'Patience,' his father answered. 'Patience and persistence.'

Then Carlitos asked his mother about his grandmother. She told him that he'd find her where he saw a cloud of dirt, because his grandmother was always sweeping, always in motion, always surrounded by dirt. But he should be careful, she said, because not all dirt clouds necessarily contained his grandmother; some dirt clouds are just dirt clouds and nothing more, while others are dirt clouds and much more besides, and that's where things get dangerous.

*

A few weeks went by before Carlitos, on the prowl for his grandfather, happened upon a dirt cloud that turned out to be his grandmother. The sight reminded him of a sparkler; dust seemed to be shooting out from the middle of it, and the specks shone in the rays of sunlight and darkened again in the shade. The dust thickened towards the cloud's centre, and Carlitos couldn't see anything in there.

Even so, he bravely resolved to go inside.

His eyes filled up quickly with dirt, and his throat started to sting.

'Grandma!' he called. 'Is that you? Where are you?'

'Of course it's me,' the woman answered with a caw. 'I'm right here. Can't you see me?'

'No, Grandma, I can't see you because I've got dust in my eyes.'

'Serves you right for messing around with dirt clouds, boy. Now, what do you want from me?'

'I want you to tell me if you know what's down there in the basement.'

'Of course I know,' his grandmother retorted, and the boy felt the broom sweeping furiously around his feet.

'What is it?' asked Carlitos eagerly.

The dirt was choking him now. He could hardly breathe, and he felt like sneezing, and his eyes hurt and his mouth was all dry.

'In the basement, there's simply—' the grandmother started saying.

'Achoo!' sneezed the boy, and he didn't hear the end of her sentence.

When he opened his mouth to ask his grandmother to kindly repeat what she'd just said, because he hadn't heard, he was overcome by a terrible coughing fit.

'Get out of here!' the old woman squawked. 'Can't you see the dirt's no good for you? Go on, scram, and never let me see you inside a dirt cloud again, or I'll whack you on the rump with this broom.'

Carlitos tried again, but he knew his grandmother was right; the dirt wasn't doing him any good. Still coughing and sneezing, his eyes full of tears, he turned and ran away.

*

He found his grandfather in a large room, at around the time of year when school was finishing up and summer was threatening to arrive, complete with buzzing mosquitoes.

Carlitos hadn't seen his grandfather for years, but he remembered him well, with his grey hair and bushy moustache, sitting at a workbench piled high with dismantled clocks, tiny screwdriver in hand. He also remembered that black thingamajig with a magnifying glass in it, which the old man held pinched in his right eye whenever he looked at the clocks.

He was surprised to find the man now lying inside a sort of glass cabinet or fish tank, his head resting on a big green pillow. He still had the lens in his right eye, and his left eye swivelled alertly in Carlitos's direction when he heard the boy come in.

The room was very big, and full of shelves heaped with clocks of all shapes and sizes. Some of them didn't even look like clocks, but more like oranges or white horses.

Carlitos thought they must make a deafening racket when they all struck the hour at the same time, but then he noticed that none of them was running, and that they all read three twenty-five.

His grandfather managed a broad grin when he saw him, despite the funnel-tipped rubber tube sticking out of his mouth. The boy stepped onto a little stool and slipped a peppermint between the old man's lips, to one side of the rubber tube. (Ever since that time he talked with his father, Carlitos always carried a bag of peppermints on his person; he'd spent all his money on them, his entire life savings, more than ten whole pesos.) His grandfather's left eye sparkled with glee; his right eye remained hidden.

Carlitos, knowing he could ask only one question, didn't hesitate to put off what really mattered to him:

'How are you, Grandpa?'

'Very well, Carlitos, very well indeed,' he answered, his smile revealing that he still had two or three teeth left.

'See you tomorrow,' said Carlitos, and off he went.

*

He had no trouble finding his grandfather's room the next day, because it was the last door in one of the hallways – the one that branched off to the left from the fireplace.

He slipped his grandfather another peppermint, then accidentally asked:

'What's that tube sticking out of your mouth for?'

'That's how I'm fed my soup,' the old man replied. 'You can't go eating soup with a spoon at my age.' Despite the tube and the peppermint, the boy heard the words very clearly. His grandfather's voice, however, sounded a long way away. 'My hands shake and I end up spilling it all, and I have a hard time remembering where my mouth is.'

Carlitos said goodbye until the next day.

*

Curiosity is a dangerous thing, because it often leads us astray. What you're all thinking is true: the new paths uncovered for us by none other than curiosity are usually a thousand times more interesting than those which curiosity led us to abandon in the first place. But notice how, in this case, curiosity leads Carlitos astray from a path he was already following out of curiosity; and, above all, notice how Carlitos, out of curiosity, squanders his bag of peppermints.

'Grandfather, why do you have that thing on your right eye?'

'It's been there for so long that when I tried to take it off I couldn't do it. And now I can't remember if I put it

there myself one day, or if I was born with it instead of
an eye.'

*

And the next day:
    'Why are the clocks stopped?'
    'So time doesn't pass.'

*

And another day (and another mint, and by now there aren't
many left):
    'And why are they all stopped at three twenty-five?'
    'Because old people die at three thirty.'

*

Finally, Carlitos comes to his senses. He doesn't ask why
this clock looks like an orange or that one like a sunset;
today he cuts straight to the matter at hand.
    'Grandpa, do you know what's in the basement?'
    'No.'

*

And another day:
    'And do you know anyone who does know?'
    'Yes.'

And another:

'Who does know what's down in the basement?'

'Your grandmother.'

*

And yet another:

'And aside from my grandmother?'

'Your father.'

*

And the next:

'Grandpa, you don't want to give me any useful information, because that way I'll keep giving you peppermints, but the one I'm giving you today is my very last one, so please, you have to answer me, because I can't get my hands on any more: tell me who knows what's down there in the basement – not my grandmother, or my father, or my mother, but someone who can and will answer when I ask.'

His grandfather thought for a few moments.

'The head gardener might give you some interesting information,' he said eventually, and it would be a long time before Carlitos saw his grandfather again.

*

The garden was enormous, and surrounded the house at the sides and back; from the house, you couldn't see the end of it, and if you ventured in among the great variety of flowers and plants, you saw it was turning into a forest, where you could observe all kinds of giant plants and trees. But as with the house, although it was so big that no one could ever know it in full, it was extremely difficult to get lost there. The paths were clear and very well marked, and there were signs with arrows pointing you where to go, whether you wanted to carry on walking or were thinking of heading home.

There were lots of gardeners – for the most part, men very short in stature. They always had their hands full, busy with a thousand different gardening-related tasks. They all wore green uniforms and on their heads were green hats (which looked like wrinkled vine leaves), and as a result, if they stood still – or moved their arms slowly – it was sometimes hard to tell them apart from the plants and trees.

Not far from the house, Carlitos came across a gardener who was squatting down, his nose almost touching the ground, and busily giving each blade of grass a gentle tug to encourage its growth. It's a highly delicate task, and requires a great deal of practice not to pull too hard (since, of course, if you pull too hard, the blade will either grow taller than the others or break) (blades of grass are perhaps too easily broken).

'Good afternoon,' said Carlitos, and the gardener jumped up like a frog and then, after turning a somersault in mid-air, landed on his back.

'Cablegram!' he shouted, furious, shutting his eyes, opening his mouth very wide and clenching his fists. 'Would you mind telling me why you had to scare me like that? You made me break a blade of grass for the first time in my life! I might lose my job over this, and then, when word gets out that I broke a blade of grass, nobody, nobody in the whole wide world, will want to hire me as their gardener; and since gardening is the only thing I know how to do, I'll probably die of hunger in no time at all, beset by poverty and disease!

'And even if I do learn another trade, through immense intellectual effort – because I admit I'm a little slow on the uptake – who's going to give me a job, in whatever new trade I happen to choose, knowing that I couldn't cut it in gardening, which is the simplest trade of all?'

Carlitos said he hadn't meant to scare him; he'd only said 'Good afternoon' to start a conversation, because he wanted to ask a question, and his parents had taught him (and he thought he also remembered his teacher telling him this at school) that it isn't polite to start a conversation without greeting the person first.

He added that if someone tried to fire the gardener over the broken blade of grass, he would simply explain what had happened and then they wouldn't be able to get rid of him.

The little man was very glad to hear this and broke into a beautiful, elaborate dance around the boy, twirling his hands and spinning round and round on tiptoe; though

I have to say that, during this dance, he failed to notice that his feet broke hundreds of blades of grass.

Eventually, the gardener, calm once more, asked Carlitos what he'd like to know.

'Are you by any chance the head gardener?' the boy asked.

The tiny man burst into uproarious laughter, showing his tongue and all his teeth, tears streaming down his cheeks. He had to throw himself to the ground, flat out, and then, grabbing his belly with his hands, he laughed and laughed, in genuine distress. He said it was all too much and he couldn't laugh any more, but then he went on like that for another few minutes. His laughter was an unbroken thread that grew weaker all the while, spooling from his lips less spontaneously with every passing moment.

'All right, all right,' he finally said, once he could talk again, getting up and leaning his back against a tall cactus (although apparently without getting pricked: gardener's secret). 'No,' he added gravely, 'I'm not the head gardener. I'm the penultimate gardener.'

'And do you know where the head gardener is?' Carlitos asked, afraid the man would start laughing again.

'He must, to be precise, be somewhere in this garden. The person most likely to know is the second gardener; I can't tell you any more than that.'

'And the second gardener – where's he?' the boy persisted.

'The third gardener should know that. Now, no more questions. To find the third gardener, you'll have to ask the fourth, and to find the fourth you'll have to ask the fifth, and so on until you make it to the very last one. That's the last one over there, painting yellow spots on the purple mushroom. He'll tell you where I am, since I'm second to last.'

'I don't need to ask that,' said Carlitos, beginning to lose his patience. 'I know perfectly well that you're right here in front of me.'

'Then ask me about the third to last gardener,' said the man, bending down again to get back to work.

'Seems to me like a very roundabout way of doing things,' Carlitos said, heading down a path and further into the garden. 'I'd be better off looking for the head gardener himself.'

*

When you're looking for something, you shouldn't even dream of finding it by chance, at least not within a set time frame. Because one of the tricks chance likes to play is hiding the very thing we're looking for and leading us to find something we're not looking for, or not looking for any more. Such, at least, is my personal experience; if the opposite is true for you, feel free to adopt whatever philosophy you like: it makes no difference to me.

But Carlitos's experience was the same as mine. The day he found his grandfather, for instance, though he was carrying the little bag of peppermints (it had become a habit by then, and he no longer even felt them in his pocket), he was going around the house on a fervent hunt for a white mouse dressed as an Eskimo. Why he'd want such a thing is another story, and would take me a whole other book to explain. I simply gave the example to support my afore-mentioned theory.

Anyway: one afternoon, Carlitos was wandering around the garden, dejected. He'd looked all over the place without seeing anyone impressive enough to be the head gardener. Only plants and flowers, and trees; and, from time to time, some silly little gardener of negligible rank.

Suddenly, he heard a feeble cry.

'Help!'

He looked around, but couldn't find whoever had yelled. Then the cry rang out again, and this time it seemed to be coming not from the north, south, east or west, but from the very place where he was standing, right by his feet.

He looked down and, sure enough, beside his right foot, he saw a puddle with a small insect swimming around in it, flailing his very long, thin legs in desperation. He was clearly about to drown, exhausted from treading water.

Carlitos bent down and put his finger in the puddle. The insect, very laboriously, managed to clamber onto it after a few attempts. Carlitos stood up and brought his finger to his eyes.

The insect, a species unknown to him, had an extremely slight, greenish body and big round eyes, and his legs – which, as I mentioned, were long and thin – now hung limply over each side of the boy's index finger.

'Phew!' said the insect, after catching his breath. 'Thanks, little man. I thought I was a goner there.'

'It's nothing, really,' answered Carlitos. He noticed the insect was panting and trying, very slowly, to get to his feet. However, he still couldn't quite manage, and his legs kept falling limply back down by his sides.

'What kind of bug are you?' the boy asked, intrigued. 'I've never seen anyone like you before.'

'I'm the only example of my species,' the insect responded with pride. 'My name is Tito, and, seeing as I'm unique, I imagine I must belong to the Tito species (or *Titus*, to be scientific about it).'

'My name's Carlitos,' said the boy in turn.

By now, Tito was standing steadily on his legs and shaking his body, the way dogs do when they get wet, to dry off more quickly.

'Tell me, Carlitos,' the insect said then. 'I'd like to return the favour. Is there anything I can do for you?'

'Oh, there's no need,' the boy replied. 'I hardly did a thing, and besides, anyone else would have done the same in my place.'

'That's what you think,' Tito said darkly. 'That's what you think, my lad. As for me, I've seen with my own eyes more than one ant drown, more than one butterfly, without anyone so much as lifting a finger. What's more, if I told you . . .'

The insect left the sentence hanging, and grimaced bitterly. Carlitos didn't feel like encouraging him, so, to change the subject, he asked if he knew how to find the head gardener.

Tito thought for a moment or two.

'Look,' he said then, 'I don't know where he is, but if you're not too scared, there's one very quick way of finding him. Of course, it's risky.'

'Tell me, tell me,' Carlitos urged.

'Before I do,' said the insect, 'I have to warn you: the head gardener is a shameless liar and he never answers questions seriously. I don't know why you want to find him, but bear in mind that he'll lie to you. It's inevitable.'

'Well, then,' said Carlitos, crestfallen, 'in that case, I'm not interested.'

Seeing how disappointed he was, Tito said:

'There is, however, a system for making him tell the truth: the head gardener might be a liar, but he doesn't have much imagination. He can't tell more than two lies in a row, you see, so if you ask him three times, he'll have to tell you the truth.'

Carlitos's face lit up.

'And finding him couldn't be easier,' the insect went on. 'See that sign next to the fountain?' Carlitos looked where the insect was pointing with one of his legs, and sure enough, there was a sign that said KEEP OFF THE GRASS. 'Well, if you go over to the fountain and step on the grass, an inspector will turn up right away and try to fine you. If you don't pay then and there, he'll take you to the head gardener to be punished. That's what I meant when I said it's risky; if you don't manage to trick him, or make an escape, I don't know what terrible punishment awaits you.'

'All the same, I'll give it a shot,' said Carlitos, who was really excited by now. The insect flapped his wings and then, satisfied with the test run, bid him farewell.

'Take care, Carlitos,' he said. 'I'll be grateful to you for the rest of my life.'

'Take care, Tito.' Carlitos waved as the insect flew off. He had to stop himself from saying, 'Send my regards to your family,' remembering that Tito was the only one of his species, and might think Carlitos was poking fun. In any case, it would have meant reminding Tito of his loneliness, and that wouldn't have been very nice.

*

He walked over to the fountain. It was very white, marble, round and full of water. In the middle was a statue of an ugly, upright fish spitting water into the air.

The fountain was surrounded by an immaculate, elegant lawn. It was a greener green than Carlitos had ever seen before; a bright and cutting green.

There was a border of red- and black-painted bricks around the lawn. The boy hesitated for a moment, then lifted his right leg and gently placed his foot on the other side.

No sooner had the sole of his shoe grazed the first blade of grass than he heard a whistle blow and some heavy footsteps making their way down the gravel path.

Carlitos took his foot off the grass and looked to his left; stomping down the path was a squat, portly fellow dressed in a grey uniform, with a grey cap on his head, puffing and panting between each blow of the whistle.

'Criminal!' he bellowed when he reached the boy. He blew his whistle again, completely unnecessarily; the noise drilled into Carlitos's ears. 'I saw you! I saw you stepping on the grass!'

'It's true,' said Carlitos.

'It's true, Mr Inspector,' the man corrected him.

'It's true, Mr Inspector,' the boy repeated.

'Good. And now you have to pay the fine. It's five hundred thousand eight hundred thousand four hundred and fifty thousand trillion million pesos.'

'How much?' Carlitos asked, wide-eyed, because he couldn't make sense of the number.

'Five hundred thousand eight hundred thousand four hundred and fifty thousand trillion million pesos,' repeated the inspector.

'I don't have that much money,' said Carlitos, checking his pockets. He took out a coin. 'Fifty cents is all I've got. That's it.'

The inspector pushed his cap forwards and scratched the back of his neck.

'Hm, I don't think that'll do,' he said, working it out, trying not to let Carlitos see him using the fingers on his left hand to count. 'I'll have to take you to the head gardener to be punished.'

'OK,' said Carlitos.

'OK, Mr Inspector,' the inspector snapped.

'OK, Mr Inspector.'

*

The inspector led Carlitos deeper into the garden, down a series of winding paths. After a while, they came to a circular area without any trees or plants. There was, however, something that *looked* like a tree in the middle of the space: namely, the head gardener.

The inspector hauled the boy towards this figure, gripping his arm hard to demonstrate his authority (a bit of theatre for his boss); he gave the necessary explanations and then, after a deep bow, went on his way.

The head gardener was, quite sincerely, a man who resembled a tree. His face was coarse, like the bark of a tree; his hair was green, like the top of a tree; his legs and feet, which he covered with a very wrinkly brown jumpsuit, were very close together and resembled the trunk of a tree, and didn't move from where they stood. His fingers were extremely long and twisted, like tree branches, and his arms were always slightly raised, and when he spoke he moved them slowly back and forth, bringing to mind a tree swaying in the breeze.

'Why did you step on the grass nineteen times?' the head gardener demanded, at last, in a tree-like voice.

'I only stepped on it once,' Carlitos answered, and then, remembering his manners, added a bit tardily, 'Mr Head Gardener.'

'Don't lie: I was told in no uncertain terms that you stepped on it twenty-three times,' he said.

'No, Mr Head Gardener. I stepped on it once and that's all.'

'Very well, then: why did you step on the grass?'

'Because,' Carlitos said, 'I wanted to talk to you, and all the lower-ranking gardeners were confusing me with their strange behaviour. If I'd followed their instructions, it would have taken such a long time to find you, and I might never have found you at all. But this way, the inspector brought me straight to you.'

'And why'd you want to see me?' the head gardener asked, taken aback, perhaps saying to himself that it was most unusual for anyone to want to see him. In his experience, it was generally the other way around.

'Ah, well' – and here Carlitos began to lie, following Tito's advice – 'you see, I've heard wonderful things about you: that you're a man of refined qualities and very wise, and that if there's anything I'd like to know, however difficult or out of the ordinary, I simply have to ask you.'

'This is all very true. Very true indeed,' the head gardener observed, clearly pleased. 'Well then, you're pardoned, because you were entirely justified in stepping on the grass. Now, tell me what you'd like to know.'

Carlitos was very relieved to have been pardoned (though he didn't notice that the head gardener had only said this once). Then, brimming with hope, he asked the question that had obsessed him for so long:

'What's in the basement of my parents' house?'

The head gardener answered right away, almost offhandedly.

'A packet of cough drops,' he said.

'What's in the basement of my parents' house?' Carlitos repeated.

'There's a lot of damp, darkness and spiderwebs, and piles of bottles and empty old demijohns, and mice and centipedes and bugs that love moisture, and the iron headboard of a dismantled bed, and a mannequin that's broken, and some stacks of old newspapers.'

This all seemed very reasonable to Carlitos and he was about to believe it; but then he remembered the insect's warning and asked again, for a third time:

'What's in the basement of my parents' house?'

The head gardener sighed and said, slowly and melancholically:

'The truth is that I don't know . . . I'm curious myself, and I often wonder about it. But it's not that important to me.'

Carlitos thought for a moment. He was sure, despite it all, that this tree-like man could be of use to him. His grandfather had said there was some connection between him and the basement, though he hadn't explained what it was.

'And do you know anyone who does know what's down there?' he asked then.

'A brother of my old lady's uncle's younger sister's brother-in-law knows,' the man answered.

Carlitos repeated the question.

'Yes,' the head gardener said, quite simply, and Carlitos didn't need to ask a third time to know what the answer would be.

He thought for another moment or two, pulling at his chin with his thumb and the knuckle of his index finger.

'Who has the key to the padlock on the basement door?' he asked at last.

'I have it, and it's very well hidden, and I'm not about to give it to anyone,' the man answered fiercely, and Carlitos almost believed him (you should have seen how earnestly this man told lies; doesn't it remind you of —? But no, that's another story too).

'Who has the key to the padlock?'

'I don't know, I swear I don't know,' the head gardener answered with tears in his eyes. Carlitos felt very sorry for him. 'If I knew, I'd ask for it and go down to the basement myself. I've always wanted to go down there.'

'Who has the key?' the boy asked a third time.

'The Iron-Swallower,' the head gardener said, angrily, because the boy had forced him to tell the truth. 'The

Iron-Swallower who lives in the well by the forest ranger's hut.'

'Thank you, Mr Head Gardener,' said Carlitos, feeling very pleased. Although he didn't know what the Iron-Swallower was, and had no idea that such a hut, or indeed a forest ranger, existed, at least he'd got a concrete answer about the basement – and, more importantly, a true one.

He bid the tree-like man a courteous farewell and got ready to leave; but before he'd taken more than two or three steps, he heard the man's booming voice:

'Henchmen! Don't let him get away! He stepped on the grass twenty-nine times and needs to be punished! Post haste!!'

Little men in suits of armour with spears in their hands started climbing down from the trees and up out of holes in the ground. They swiftly formed a squadron, captained by the tallest among them – though he was no taller than the boy. There were three guards in the second row, five in the third, seven in the fourth, nine in the fifth, and eleven in the sixth. Carlitos was very surprised, because the head gardener had pardoned him; but then he remembered that he'd only pardoned him once, which meant it was a lie. He bolted in panic, as the spears of the little men – who were running after him – began to rain down around his body.

'Don't let him get away!' the head gardener cried, and his menacing tree voice spurred the boy to run even faster.

*

He ran, and ran, and ran.

*

He ran, and ran, and ran.

*

He ran, but he felt like he was always in the same place. Given his fear of getting caught, and the pressure of the chase, Carlitos wasn't able to pay much attention to the details, but, after running for a long time, he came to the conclusion that he had been running in circles, and always around the head gardener (who, incidentally, was still screaming his head off).

And yet the boy had followed the signs, the ones painted neatly on wooden arrows, which said TO THE HOUSE, TO THE POND, TO THE PARK, etc. He'd simply followed all the arrows marked TO THE HOUSE and run without worrying about anything else, but eventually he understood.

'It's the signs,' he muttered to himself, and felt very, very, very tired. 'Signs are supposed to keep you from getting lost, but these ones are only here to confuse you.' So he stopped following the signs, and went on running wherever they didn't point.

*

'Hey!' someone shouted. 'Hey, kid! Over here!'

Carlitos looked and saw a clearing in the trees; another circular space, completely covered in little flowers. Some were yellow, others purple, and they were arranged in marvellous, incomprehensible patterns.

At the very centre of the circle, a diminutive man was sitting in mid-air and beckoning to him.

Carlitos approached. The man was no taller than the guards and had a long white beard. He stood up, made as if he were opening an invisible door, then took Carlitos by the hand and led him through it, before closing it behind him.

'So they're after you,' he said serenely, as if commenting on a perfectly ordinary occurrence. Carlitos, who was very, very, very tired and out of breath, kept looking nervously over his shoulder. And sure enough, right then, all the guards came racing down the path, shouting and hurling their spears.

The men looked in their direction but didn't seem to see them, and continued on their way.

The boy reached out his hands, but he didn't touch anything; there was obviously no door there, nor any walls.

'This is the garden's loony bin,' the little man announced, sitting back down in the air and crossing his right leg over his left.

'I don't understand,' said Carlitos. 'I don't understand a thing.'

'What would you like to know about?' the man asked, eyeing him fondly.

'Everything. All this,' Carlitos murmured. 'You just opened a door that doesn't exist, then you closed it again. The guards ran by and didn't see me, even though I could see them perfectly well. And now you're sitting in mid-air, telling me this is a loony bin.'

'That's correct,' the little man replied, producing a lit pipe from inside his clothes and taking a puff. 'But, please, make yourself at home.' And he knocked a couple of times on the air, which sounded like wood, then gestured to a spot next to where he was sitting. 'You're exhausted. Come, take a load off for a while.'

With a suspicious look, Carlitos reached out and tried to knock on the air himself, but it didn't make a sound, and he didn't feel like he'd touched anything.

'No, no,' said the man. 'If you don't have faith, you won't be able to sit down.'

Carlitos didn't want to offend him, and so pretended to take his word for it. But he wasn't convinced, and when he tried to sit beside the little man, he fell and landed on the floor.

'Let me explain,' the man said. 'I used to be like them – just another henchman. I had to spend my days in a tree, waiting for the head gardener to yell for us to chase someone.

'It was extremely dull, and unrewarding besides. Mostly we had to chase good people who hadn't done anything more than step on the grass or ask the butterflies a question.

In the end I got fed up. I said I didn't want to be a henchman any more and asked to be transferred to gardening.

'Then everyone said I was crazy, because henchmen get paid a much higher salary and are very respected – plus, in gardening you have to work much harder, all day long (and sometimes at night, too). So they locked me up in this cell.

'A lot of time passed. The walls began to crumble, and no one bothered to rebuild them. I feel fantastic here. I don't have to chase anyone, the guards bring me food, and I've got everything I need. Over time, they saw the walls were disappearing, but didn't want to say anything because then the head gardener would have made them build another cell, and everyone knows the guards are a bunch of loafers.

'And so, even though the cell hasn't existed for many, many years, it goes on existing for them, and for me, and its existence is so expedient for us that we can still see it and touch it. I myself, as you'll surely have noticed, can sit comfortably on a wooden stool that fell to pieces a long time ago.'

'And why didn't they see me?' asked Carlitos, who still didn't entirely understand.

'They did see you, actually, but they didn't believe in you. If they did, they would have to admit the cell doesn't exist and build a new one. So instead they chose to see the cell and, since they can't see through walls, they didn't see you.

'No, they'll be running around for a while now. In the end, they'll get tired and go back to the head gardener with some story or other: that they lost sight of you because, just like that, you turned into a bird and flew off, or that you climbed up on a giant lobster and it carried you, leaping, all the way to the moon.'

'And the boss will believe them?'

'Nope. But if he doesn't believe them, he'll have to punish them, after carrying out a thorough investigation, which he finds rather tiresome. So he'll pretend to believe them.'

At that moment the guards, who were getting a little weary by now, came back along the path. Once again, they looked right at them, but continued on their way.

'See what I mean?' said the man triumphantly, pointing at them.

'And what about you?' asked Carlitos, who still had his doubts. 'How can you see them, but at the same time believe in the cell so much that you're able to sit on a stool that doesn't exist?'

'Well,' the man smiled, taking a few puffs of his pipe. 'That's the trick, right there.' He scratched his head. 'I've never really known how I do it, but that's the trick. I must really be crazy after all. It's not for nothing I'm locked up in this loony bin.'

'But don't you ever leave?' asked the boy, because it seemed sad for such a nice man to have spent all his time locked up for so many years.

'Oh, yes,' the man said enthusiastically. 'I leave very, very, very often. I just have to be back by noon, which is when they bring me my food. Yesterday, it just so happens, I was over at the house of my friend the forest ranger.'

'The forest ranger!' Carlitos exclaimed, and immediately asked to hear more.

EXTREMELY BRIEF STORY ABOUT THE FOREST RANGER
AS TOLD TO CARLITOS BY THE LITTLE MAN WITH THE
WHITE BEARD IN A CLEARING IN THE WOODS

Many, many, many, many years ago, the woods in your garden were very, very, very, very, very, very, very, very big. Everyone knows that very, very, very, very, very, very, very, very big woods need forest rangers, so a hut was built and a forest ranger put inside it.

Time passed, and the woods grew smaller, because men needed wood to build wardrobes. People had taken to buying lots of clothes, and the wardrobes they had weren't big enough any more.

Eventually, the woods were reduced to the size they are now, leaving the rest as nothing but an empty field. The forest ranger's hut remained, then, in the middle of a huge empty field, and the forest ranger had to retire, because no one wanted to pay him to look after a very, very, very, very, very, very, very small forest.

Now he lives with his wife, children and grandchildren, and his great-grandchildren and his great-great-grandchildren's great-great-grandchildren on that red mushroom near the pond, and spends his time reading the paper and drinking maté.

*

'And is there a well next to the hut?' Carlitos asked.

'Yes, but it's dry. The Iron-Swallower lives down there now.'

'And what's the Iron-Swallower?'

'You'd never guess,' the little man replied. 'He's a creature that swallows iron.'

'So he swallowed the key to the basement,' Carlitos concluded.

'No doubt about it,' the man said. 'No doubt at all. He loves a good key. But if you want to get it back, you just have to offer him something made of iron that he likes even more, then he'll throw the key right up and give it to you.'

'And what would he like more than a basement key?' asked Carlitos.

'Ah!' said the little man, letting his arms fall to his sides. 'Nobody knows. You'll have to find out for yourself.'

Carlitos stood up, thanking him profusely for saving him from the guards, and for the conversation, which had been so edifying. The man shook his hand and told him to visit whenever he wanted.

Carlitos promised to come back one day, and waved goodbye, but when he tried to leave, he walked straight into a wall.

'Oh!' the little man hurried over, alarmed. 'Are you all right?'

'Yes, yes,' said Carlitos, touching his nose, because it hurt. Now, ever so faintly, he could make out an extremely old, dilapidated wall, which was almost transparent, but without a doubt perfectly solid.

The little man opened the make-believe door. Carlitos stepped through it, saying goodbye once more, and headed on his way.

In order to find the empty field, all he had to do was walk in any direction EXCEPT WHERE THE SIGNS WERE POINTING.

*

It took him several days to find the forest ranger's hut. It was located, just as the little man had said, in the middle of a huge, desolate field. Wherever you looked, out there, you saw nothing but field; the grass was withered and sallow, very different from the kind the gardeners tended, and there weren't any trees, plants or animals to be seen.

The hut was almost in ruins, with only a few boards still standing. The well was painted white with lime, and there was a bucket on a rope hanging from the pulley wheel. Carlitos looked over the edge and shouted down:

'Mr Iron-Swallower!'

A cavernous voice answered almost straight away, saying something Carlitos couldn't understand, whether because it had used a word he didn't know, or because the echo in the well had distorted the sound.

'My name's Carlitos,' said the boy, 'and I want the key to the basement of my parents' house. I've brought some merchandise to trade.'

(Along the way, Carlitos had picked up some objects he thought looked appealing.)

The voice boomed again. This time he thought it was saying, 'Come on down!' but he wasn't sure. Since he didn't want to aggravate the Iron-Swallower, he decided to climb into the well instead of repeating the question – whose answer, he was sure, he wouldn't understand.

So he untied the rope from one of the posts holding up the pulley, and slowly let the bucket down. Then he tied the rope to the post again, took hold of it and slid carefully to the bottom of the well.

It was very dark, but after a short while, his eyes got used to the gloom and he made out the Iron-Swallower.

He was a transparent, formless creature, like an amoeba, with just one enormous eye that was always moving around inside his body, and in the middle of that jelly-like mass there was an untidy heap of iron – the Iron-Swallower's lunch, no doubt.

That animal, or whatever he was, had no arms, or legs, or head, or anything else; just a shapeless body, and that eye of his.

'Good afternoon,' Carlitos said, trying not to let the

creature notice how terribly frightened he was, and then repeated his offer of a trade.

The Iron-Swallower stared at him, moving his eye to the centre of his body and fixing it there. That vacant, motionless gaze, unblinking and bereft of any tenderness, made Carlitos feel even more afraid than before.

'So, what is it you've brought me?' the Iron-Swallower said at last. (His voice sounded exactly like a record playing at a very slow speed.)

Carlitos reached into his pocket, puzzled by how this creature could talk without a mouth, and produced a handsome penknife. He placed it in the palm of his hand and held it close to the Iron-Swallower's eye.

'Bah!' the creature said. 'Not interested. That's stainless steel.'

So Carlitos went on reaching into his pockets and pulling things out: ball bearings, forks, corkscrews, bottle openers, scissors, a key, another key, needles for unclogging stoves, caps from fizzy-drink bottles, yet another key, a dog chain, and lots of other stuff.

'I'm not interested in any of it,' the Iron-Swallower said. 'Absolutely none. Tin, acrylic, manganese, plaster, tin, tin, tin.'

Finally, the boy gave up.

'I don't have anything else to offer you,' he said, and his eyes began to fill with tears.

'Oh, I see,' said the Iron-Swallower, rather nastily. 'Little crybaby wants to have it his way.'

This made the boy absolutely furious, and he couldn't hold back his sobs. The Iron-Swallower got frightened and said:

'Enough, enough! Tears are very bad for me. In fact, that's all I'm afraid of – tears and seawater. They're salty, and sooner or later they rust the iron in my stomach, which gives me awful cramps.'

Since Carlitos wouldn't stop crying, the creature gave a sort of hiccup, and the key to the basement soared out, as if by magic, and landed in the boy's right hand.

'Now get out of here,' the Iron-Swallower said, and Carlitos thanked him and started climbing up the rope.

*

This story seems endless, I know, and perhaps it is; I'm not trying to complicate it artificially, however, but rather to stick strictly to the truth of what happened. It's not my fault if the events and their ramifications are complex; I'm doing my best to describe them clearly and concisely, but I can't distort the truth, as so many people do, not even for the sake of my delightful readers.

Readers who, on reading these lines, will wonder indignantly: 'So why not write something else? Something shorter, or simpler? Nobody forced him to tell this story.'

Such criticism may seem entirely justified, but the fact is that I *did* try telling other stories – and at first I thought this one would turn out shorter, prettier and simpler – but my stories are always, always, always long and complicated.

And it's not my fault. It's not my fault if these things happened to the characters. It's not my fault if the rope in the well broke . . . (It was a very old rope.)

*

Carlitos fell, thankfully not from very high up, and landed right next to the Iron-Swallower.

'You nearly crushed me!' the creature howled, in a rage, and now Carlitos was crying again, because he felt like he'd never make it out of that well.

'Listen,' the IS said (IS = Iron-Swallower; I'll be using this abbreviation from now on, because maybe Carlitos really won't ever make it out of that well, and it would be tedious to write such a long name over and over again), speaking slowly and with great kindness and patience. 'You'll never get out of here now, because the rope's broken. You might as well stop crying, so you don't do me any harm, and get used to the idea. I know a whole bunch of thrilling stories, and lots of riddles, maths problems and puzzles. You won't get bored, you'll see.

'Have you heard the one about the Hysterical Paperboy? It's a riot. So, one day . . .'

But Carlitos didn't want to stay; outside, it seemed, were things far more interesting than any story the IS could tell him; so he started climbing again, this time supporting his feet on little ledges and spaces between the bricks where the mortar had fallen off.

But he soon slipped back down.

The IS was livid.

'Everyone thinks it's so much fun to fall down right on top of me!' he shouted. 'Sure, I'm squishy and I cushion the impact! But I don't like it, not one bit – you could kill me with that stupid game. So I'm left with no choice but to eat you, even though I don't like meat. My favourite food is iron.'

And with these words he began to spread out across the bottom of the well, as if he were made of thick, rubbery water. He grew so thin that you could see everything inside him; but Carlitos was very frightened and couldn't stop to examine all the extraordinary objects the IS had in his belly. He managed to make out a doorknob and something like the wheel of a tram, then started climbing the side of the well as fast as he could.

'Dammit!' shouted the IS, who used an atrocious vocabulary when he got angry. 'You're going to fall on me and pop my eye out – and it's the only one I've got!'

Then he shrank once more and pressed himself against the wall opposite the one Carlitos was climbing.

Many times the boy fell back down to the bottom, and many times the IS began to spread himself out, only to shrink back when the boy started climbing again.

'I'm getting tired of this game,' said the IS at last. 'It's fine, I won't try to eat you. Stop climbing and come over here next to me. I've got a riddle for you: supposing a

Knot-Untier and an Elephant-Smasher – each furnished with the tools of his respective trade – were to meet in a clearing in the forest and get into a fight, how many hours would it take the Knot-Untier to beat the Elephant-Smasher, if the latter is tired after dancing all night at the Scissor-Hider's party?'

But Carlitos barely heard the last part of the question, because he'd managed to reach the top of the well, and soon he was outside. He liked riddles, but this one was all about very strange people, people no doubt known only to the Iron-Swallower and his world. As for Carlitos, he had more important matters to attend to.

*

It was many, many years before Carlitos made it home.

You see, when he got out of the well . . . but no; that story would take so many pages and so much time for me write out with all the details that I'd get completely distracted from the business of the basement, and I'd be an old man before I could pick up the thread again, and maybe I'd even die. Let's just say, then, that many, many years went by.

*

Things had changed a great deal. Carlitos was no longer Carlitos, but Carlos. He had a moustache and three strands of grey in his hair. He found that his parents' house was no longer surrounded by a beautiful garden, but by strange constructions in which strange people were doing truly strange things; and inside the house there was no one.

*

He walked into every room and they were all empty, completely empty. Just one – the thirtieth in the third hallway – had a blue and red marble in it, hidden in a hole in the floor, which he'd lost when he was a boy.

*

I stood facing the padlocked door. I reached into my pocket and took out the key the Iron-Swallower had given me. When I turned it in the padlock, the lock popped open. I removed the padlock, turned the door handle, pulled, and the door creaked open: in front of me were four or five steps of a wooden staircase. The rest lay in the darkest of darks.

*

I light the candle I brought along for this very purpose, and then, after hesitating for just a moment or two, start walking down the stairs.

August 1966–August 1967
Tr. KS and AM

THAT GREEN LIQUID

For Jaime

There's a knock at the door. I'm not expecting anyone, so I'm surprised by the knocking. Still, I open up.

It's a green-eyed girl in a uniform. She smiles, shows me a briefcase and says:

'May I come in? This is a free at-home demonstration.'

Without thinking, I step aside and in she comes, opening her briefcase. She takes out a duster and a bottle, but I don't notice that yet; she's followed in by a clown, who does a handstand in the middle of the room, and there are more people waiting outside.

The girl wets the duster with the contents of the bottle – a green liquid – and starts wiping the table, rubbing slowly in circular motions. A couple of tightrope walkers have come in now and they're doing marvellous tricks; one involves swinging from the chandelier, turning a full somersault in mid-air and landing on their feet with a salute. But my attention is taken up by the animal tamer who strides in with a lion and tiger (whose stomachs growl alarmingly), and then the equestrian standing on her horse's back, and the camels and the giraffe and the elephant – this last getting stuck halfway in, though the ringmaster has opened both doors especially. The elephant looks rather sorry for itself while the trainer and the clown push it back out, to dislodge it; they then push it inside again, at a slight angle, and manage to get it through.

Last of all is the stunt rider, who zooms in on his motorbike at top speed, making an infernal racket. He rides all over the walls and even on the ceiling.

I go to the girl and tell her I've seen quite enough of her at-home demonstration, that I'm no longer interested, and besides, I'm not about to make any purchases; that she's wasting her time, and I mine.

She's not annoyed. Instead she smiles, breaks off her circular motions, packs up her things, says goodbye and leaves. As she's going down the stairs, I lean out and yell after her:

'And take your circus with you, for God's sake!'

'My circus?' she asks, astonished. 'What are you talking about? Those people weren't with me.'

Tr. AM

THE BOARDING HOUSE

Time and again, especially in the early days (when I thought the move marked my first steps towards independence, and used to gaze, enthralled, on propitious nights, through the narrow rectangular window above the wardrobe, at the passage of the moon – which on rare occasions I could observe from the bed, in a comfortable horizontal position, before falling asleep bathed in that thick, milky light, and dreaming of spiral staircases, naked women and cabbage patches; mostly, however, it was necessary, after first moving the little table and placing the wooden stool on top, to climb onto the roof of the wardrobe and often even stick my head partway out of the window – and had yet to learn, through unfortunate experiences – such as the night when I was doodling on a piece of paper and subconsciously sensed the approach of a small dark shape, seeing it out of the corner of my eye but not quite believing it, and then, when the impression reached my conscious plane, realising with horror that it was a spider of considerable proportions, and that I had no choice, despite my feelings of disgust, and

85

even guilt, but to squash it with one end of the T-square which had been hanging, until that point for purely decorative purposes, from a nail in the wall; I felt a crunch followed by something soft and the little body shrivelled up, but I had no time to recover because from under the right-hand door, which led to the next room along, a platoon of similar arachnids was advancing towards me in a V-formation, obliging me to grit my teeth and apply the same T-square procedure to each of those thirty-six specimens, which drove me to the heights of madness and left me in a state beyond nausea and vomiting, and the next day, on returning to my room after a night spent wandering the streets, gathering the strength to go back and face the thirty-seven corpses, I found my neighbour awaiting me, a Japanese man who explained that his spiders were harmless, and indeed trained, and had escaped when he wasn't paying attention from the jar where he kept them and turned up in my room not, as I had imagined, on the warpath, but rather in search of an audience to dazzle with the miraculous acrobatic abilities he had drilled into them through years of patient work, following which he called me a murderer and a monster, and I had to plead ignorance and fear as justification for my act of vandalism, and promise, in order to calm him down, that I would join him on future expeditions through the wetlands in search of new specimens, with the aim of collecting a suitable number to form another squad – of the existence of the neighbours, about whom I should add, in the interests of fairness, that the Japanese man is far from the most troublesome, paling as he does in comparison, for example, with the scientist, who has procured, without the involvement of a human male, but rather by electrically stimulating an egg, the abnormally large adult foetus that has lived in a glass jar for more than four years and still not officially been born, and into which, on the basis that in a couple of years' time, when it's finally born, it will be found to have new and longed-for sensory powers, he instils, daily and indefatigably, by reading aloud from highly detailed texts in such fields as poetry, mathematics, philosophy and history, an understanding and sensibility far superior to the average, which will allow it to use its extraordinary abilities for the good of humanity, becoming a kind of new Christ, as the wise man says, who will stir the dead consciousness of all the individuals in this world who march blindly in their droves towards full automation, and I, out of moral duty, must help not only with the reading, taking the scientist's place when his eyes give out, but also with the careful feeding of the foetus at specific times, using a purpose-built device to pump the nutritious liquid down the half-natural, half-plastic umbilical cord; or with the old spy, whose room is on one of the floors above mine, and who, neither in bad faith nor for any practical purpose, but rather out of simple curiosity, most likely stemming from her provincial origins, closely monitors if not all then at least the vast majority of the boarders' movements, gathering her information through blackmail based on previously acquired data, as well as through her astonishing network of microphones, wires, recording equipment, transmitters and other state-of-the-art gadgets, all cunningly concealed, sometimes in a pot of forget-me-nots, or an octopus-style clothes airer attached to the bathroom tiles, and using, for both the routine spying work and the more complex technical tasks such as installing and operating the equipment, a team of special agents that includes almost all of us; or with the neighbour opposite, who has embroiled me, after first winning me over with some packs of filter-tipped cigarettes he gets on the black market, in his clandestine affair with the buxom blonde, bringing her regularly, and far more often than I'd like, to my room, from which I am then *ipso facto* ejected, obliged to loiter in alleyways and cafés and then knock on my own door before going back in, which brings on a range of emotional states that are all very damaging to my nerves, along with other feelings, first and foremost more guilt, because I think of his noble, pretty, self-sacrificing wife, whom I feel partly responsible for harming through my complicity with her husband, an arrangement I'm not entirely sure how I entered into, though it all began with a favour, man to man, sealed with a private wink that I didn't want to admit to either understanding or condoning, and which I never suspected would become a regular, almost ritual event; or with the other neighbour, from down the hall, whom I first

greeted one evening when I'd had a few too many, leading
to an exchange of pleasantries that culminated in the daily
ordeal, the result of her compassion for a single man, of
having her sweep my floor and even tidy my papers, and
the other ordeal, which, though weekly, is no less irritating,
of being forced to partake, as an attentive, appreciative and
well-disposed listener, in her appalling piano renditions of
Chopin, though I must admit I'm not impartial to the pol-
onaise – and when I was still too naïve to suppose that, far
from achieving that coveted independence from certain
unnecessary responsibilities that go hand in hand with
family ties, I would instead end up bound by these snares
that I don't know if I'll ever be able to break, because even
my office job – on which, not long ago, I pinned my hopes
of freedom – failed roundly in that regard, only distracting
me from my search for effective solutions to my problem,
if any exist, and plunging me into another set of responsibilities that were, if such a thing is possible, even more alien
to me than these, but which I fortunately managed to shake
off in the end, first by feigning illness and then by simply
ceasing to show up; I could no longer bear all that traipsing
up and down gloomy corridors, carrying papers whose contents I mostly knew nothing about, not that knowing would
have done me any good, or the empty hours over mugs of
coffee, listening to the other employees' banal conversations, conversations they thought themselves very clever
to be having, instead of getting on with their work,

whenever the boss was away, without seeing that they were still growing tired and old, just as they were while using their typewriters and calculators, with the same predetermined future of a pot belly, premature baldness and a grave decorated with flowers for a while), when making the journey from the front door to my room (which involves corridors that are damp when it rains and sometimes when it doesn't, as well as creaky wooden staircases, ladders, chicken coops with an intolerable stench and dangerously slippery floors – thanks to the chicken shit – and pitch-dark tunnels I have to go through on my knees, and which I never go through with an easy mind because as I put down each hand I think of the Japanese man's spiders and worry I might encounter a soft hairy body instead of cement or earth, and of which two memories stand out in particular, one foolish – namely when my head, as I was making my way through a tunnel, collided with another, which belonged to a man, part of whose journey from his room to the street intersects with my own, although he lives on another floor, and we both stubbornly refused, faced with the impossibility, since the tunnel was so narrow, of continuing along our respective paths, to be the one to reverse, for all that we each claimed urgent business and asserted rights based on who had covered the most ground or was older or younger, even eventually coming to blows, and then having no choice but to reverse, after two hours of patient struggle, because of my adversary's superior strength – and a second, which was more pleasant, at least at first – though with very sad consequences for me, if not for her – and came about under similar circumstances, only this time involving a lady, whom I was unfortunately unable to identify afterwards, whether because she'd taken a wrong turn that day and then couldn't find her way back there, or because she was hiding from me on purpose, even to the extent of changing her perfume, that distinctive, exotic scent for which I have searched the hair of every woman here in vain, it being the only possible means of identification, since the tunnel was so dark I couldn't see her, and who has ripped my heart to shreds with the memory of those caresses I will never feel again, of her body trembling in my arms, of the taste of her lips, the heat of her breasts, the feeling of true love which I have never known since, and the unbearable doubts that arise automatically with every woman I see, only to turn to despair when I think of the girl in the basement, whom I regularly run into in the dining room, and who I have learnt is pregnant and hiding her child's name from her parents, though the perfume she uses doesn't match the one I remember; and also involves passing through occupied rooms, which I find particularly awkward when I'm unable to respect the human right to privacy, having caught the occupants countless times in copulation, masturbation and various sexual perversions and revolting acts, since the doors have no key or lock of any kind, and although at first I used to knock discreetly before daring to go in, I soon realised that the occupants liked to pretend not to hear, and after a while, when I decided to dispense with all those hours of waiting and open the door regardless a few seconds after knocking, they set about blocking my way with piles of furniture or other obstacles, obliging me to turn to the landlady, that plump woman of indeterminate age, and report this far from friendly treatment, threatening to leave her boarding house and explaining that anyone else in my place would do the same thing and more, thereby tarnishing, slowly but irreversibly, her establishment's reputation; this made her listen to my complaints and use her influence to ensure that my path was left clear, meaning there's now no trouble in that respect and the inhabitants of those rooms, though hating me in one sense for disturbing their private activities, at the same time understand that it's absurd to make this a personal vendetta, and we've managed to stay on good terms despite the fact that, while some of them have even grown rather fond of me, through a curious split-ting or duality they continue to hate the boarding-house resident who passes through their rooms, who is also me; I refused to comply with their requests and fix a time for passing through, since that would place unacceptable limits on my freedom, so instead they had the idea of working out the minimum possible time that would elapse before I went back through their rooms after I'd already been through once, be that on my way out or returning to my room, and making use of those carefully timed intervals of safety to carry out their perverse, human or grotesque acts; with some malice and, I admit, morbid curiosity – although there were of course other motives – I have dedicated part of my life in this boarding house to making my circuitous journey at different hours of the day in order to interrupt those activities, often doubling back and returning to their rooms when they're not expecting it, though I repeat: not only out of morbid curiosity or malice, but also because, not ultimately finding in my own room the spiritual peace and solitude I crave, and unable to resign myself to spending most of my time outside the boarding house, being as I am very sensitive to the aggressions of the outside world, the journey between the outside and my room has, for some months now, taken on a value of its own; it has filled many hours of my life and become an activity in itself, a vital exercise that I can't carry out either in my room or outside the boarding house, and which has helped me to relax or distracted me from my mix of claustro- and agoraphobia), I have wondered if this enormous building – far more enormous than the distracted passer-by (or indeed the attentive passer-by) would expect, on observing from the pavement the narrow entrance, squeezed in between two large trading houses – could possibly have been designed for its current purpose, because it seems hard to believe the architects had this in mind, and then I think perhaps they were planning a post office or special needs school instead, and the closer I look the more convinced I become, since any purpose ascribed to this building, however absurd, would surely be more fitting than the current one; and when I inspect (as I did at first in the hope of discovering a new, more direct route to my room, though now, having abandoned that possibility, I do it simply because I find it fascinating) other areas that aren't on my usual route, and see the disorder in several parts of the building, the uneven floors, the staircases that end in insurmountable walls, the squalor in some regions and the luxury in others, the overcrowding of dozens of families into a single room (while sometimes one person will occupy several rooms without any apparent need), or the disparity in the rates people pay, I conclude that not only is the boarding house very badly built, or built for other purposes, but it is also very badly run; that the land-lady isn't up to the task, and if things carry on the way they're going and if, instead of finding that independence here which is so essential to me, I grow ever more entangled in this horrible mess (which has grown considerably more complicated since the installation, by some inscrutable men following orders from an as yet unidentified source, of that telephone which is completely unnecessary to me, because I have no one to call, nor am I expecting calls from anyone else – and the only reason I'm not working tirelessly to have it removed, or indeed cutting the cord, is that once, not long after it was installed, I took a call from a woman who asked my name just before the line cut out, and while that hasn't happened again since I live in hope – though I do, at desolate moments, dial the number for that voice which tries in vain to sound aloof and lacking in feminine charms while telling you the time; but after it had rung repeatedly, thanks to wrong numbers from people looking for Martita or the Rodríguez family, my neighbours caught on and began spreading the word that a telephone was available for making and even receiving calls free of charge, and it wasn't long before I had to move my bed and table to one side, against the wall, to make room for that spiral-shaped queue of people who wait their turn patiently day and night and stop me from concentrating on reading or any other activity, distracted and tormented as I am by snatches of one-sided conversations, and though they relate to trivial matters I know nothing about, all too often I find myself trying to piece together what's being said, filling in the phrases heard only by the ear pressed to the receiver with phrases from my own imagination, which then merge with the various conversations that the people in line conduct among themselves, in addition to eating and even sleeping as they wait their turn, and that cacophony of voices pursues me all the way into my dreams, whether because it's really there or because my mind, after working ceaselessly during the day to supply the missing phrases, continues to do so obsessively, of its own accord, as I sleep), I will be forced to pack my bags and leave – though I'm well aware of the extremely challenging housing situation, and the near impossibility of finding anywhere better – with no thought for the consequences, and with no idea where destiny will lead me; because, quite honestly, I can't take it here much longer.

Tr. AM

THE STIFF CORPSE

For Sammy

I opened the wardrobe to look for a tie, and the stiff corpse landed on top of me.

'Who left that there?' I yelled, furious. The elderly maid, shamefaced, cowered in the space under the stairs. 'Was it you?' I asked, threatening to hit her between the eyes with the end of the broom handle.

'No, sir,' she replied. I hit her with the broom regardless, sliding the handle over my flexed left thumb and then taking the shot with my right hand, quick and precise. She collapsed with a noise like a billiard ball. Maybe she did have something to do with it.

'It doesn't even look like anyone,' I murmured, inspecting the stranger lying face down on the bedroom floor, its feet still inside the wardrobe. 'Although perhaps' – and here I tilted the head to one side with my shoe – 'perhaps there's a hint of Aunt Encarnación about the profile . . .' I thought it might be some long-forgotten dead relative (I don't open the wardrobe very often).

'No,' I went on, though the shape of the chin looked extremely familiar. 'It's not my cousin Alfredo, or Uncle Juan.' Then I hung the corpse from a nail on the wall and left it there, studying it from time to time.

'Hey, you,' I heard a voice say to me one afternoon, when I was alone in the bedroom. I looked around but couldn't see another living thing besides the stiff corpse, still stiff and hanging on the wall.

'Yes?' I inquired.

'Look in the mirror,' it said, in the strange voice of the dead.

Somewhat alarmed, I went over to the wardrobe and tried to see my reflection in the mirror on the door.

'Hey!' I shouted. 'Hey, hey, hey! What happened to my reflection?' I demanded, distressed, because the mirror faithfully showed everything in the room, with the exception of my body.

'You don't understand a thing. You never do,' the stiff corpse said, with a silent laugh and a mocking sneer, before smoothly unhooking itself from the nail and advancing towards me, stretching.

'You?' I asked, and the word seemed to have no meaning. The corpse (no longer so stiff) came even closer, placed both hands on my chest and shoved me hard in the direction of the wardrobe. I didn't feel the collision with the mirror, but I found myself in a world where everything was tragically altered, the left on the right, the right on the left, etc. I saw the corpse taking great strides about the room, on the other side, and I had no choice but to do the same, though I'm feeling very tired now, and that man never stops walking.

Tr. AM

JELLY

For Tola and Milka

The first puff of smoke made me nauseous. Saliva filling my mouth, I looked for some free space on the floor where I could stub out my cigarette, then I got to my feet. There were grumbles, as usual; I took no notice. In the bathroom I turned on the tap, and only a tiny trickle of water came out; I splashed my eyes and tried to rinse my mouth, but the nasty taste was still there. I went outside.

The sky was getting lighter. It was cold. I zipped up my jacket; there was some bread and chocolate in the pockets, and I nibbled a few pieces. My lips got dirty, from the chocolate. I wiped them on my sleeve, but the feeling lingered.

I stood on the street corner for a while. The shop was closed, and the wooden shutters aren't bad to lean on. I thought I could doze a bit when they all left the park, though I don't find it easy in the sun; besides, the park is never completely empty, and I prefer not to be seen. Then I gave up on the idea of sleep. 'I'd better stop thinking,' I said to myself, 'and find something to do.'

*

Anselmo was already at work on the hole. He was surprised to see me so early.

'I woke up suddenly, alone,' I said, and added that I'd come to help. He passed me a shovel no bigger than my hand, without any comment, though he watched me out of the corner of his eye. We started digging, in silence, me filling a bucket with earth and him emptying it when it was full. The sun came out and the day grew unbearably hot. I considered stopping but carried on for a while, out of habit, and besides, I was scared of getting bored. Then I told him I was going. He said tomorrow they'd hit rock and have to use the drill, so I should stop by. I said maybe, non-committal. He said I was mad if I expected to be paid for digging that measly bit of earth, and I laughed and said I'd done it for fun. All the same, he gave me a little packet, something wrapped in greasy brown paper.

*

Around midday I went to the esplanade, less to see the blind people than to get some shade, though the blind people are funny, the way they lead each other around and then break into fights. Not many people were watching; it gets depressing after a while. They're dirty, most of them are naked, and I find naked men disgusting. There are some women as well, but not many. They're all wearing clothes and they're very thin.

One group started fighting over a woman and I felt bad and went off to the ruins. It's a place I love and it's always empty; with a few exceptions, people don't know how to appreciate ruins, and the place is so big you can walk and walk without seeing a soul. Since I don't have any money it isn't dangerous, though Ruth told me someone was killed there a few days ago, and not for their cash.

I untied the package and found it was a milanesa between two slices of bread. I was glad Anselmo had given me food, because I didn't feel like going all that way and waiting around. I ate leaning against a wall that I like, which has marks where some steps used to be. It looks like the staircase is still there, only invisible. The wallpaper's quite silly, a repeated fleur-de-lys, though when it went mouldy and started to peel it became a bit more interesting. I looked for some shade among the piles of rubble and fell asleep.

*

The sun moved and now it was shining on my head. I woke up in a bad mood; I could have done with more sleep. My eyes were puffy and I needed to wash my face, but it was impossible. I spat on my hands and smeared saliva around my eyes. It made them worse, stickier.

I headed for the fountain (imagining it would still be dry), because I thought by then the circle would be forming. Patting my pocket, I checked the coin was still there.

*

'You haven't paid in two days,' said Hobbler, and I held out the coin. Then he carried on talking, while I sat down on the rock. 'He chose to go into the jelly,' he said, 'rather than let go of one lousy peso. Disgusting. These people disgust me.' And he spat on the ground, with genuine hatred.

Silence fell, and I knew, I swear I knew, what Dwarf was about to ask me. (He's not a dwarf, in fact, but very tall.)

'And your Llilli?' he demanded, with a stupid grin. 'Have you seen your Llilli?'

I scraped the ground with the toe of my shoe and muttered an insult, my head bowed. There was no need to remind me. He apologised and said he hadn't been winding me up, that he'd been asking to be nice, that we all have a Llilli tucked away in some corner of our heart; I told him to shut up or change the subject, then Ulises fudged the order of the circle and passed me the maté gourd. No one objected, and Worm started talking about cigarettes; he said we could go on another group raid, since the last one had been such a success. Personally, I still had a few cigarettes left, but I gave my approval because I wanted something to do. I hate inactivity, it makes me think.

There was an argument, and eventually we agreed to go the next day, and to widen the scope to include alcohol as well. I liked the sound of that, because I needed alcohol, and because I saw some unease in the circle. I thought something might yet be done with the group. It's infuriating to see people who have so much in common going to waste.

*

They'd made me think about Llilli, and I didn't want that. I end up stewing for hours and always conclude that there's no way of finding her. And if I did find her, what then? At which point I laugh and, when I can, I get drunk.

*

Too early to return to the room. I could go and take a look at the centre, but on foot. I'd spent my last coin and didn't feel like getting hold of another; only if the opportunity arose. It's a question of inspiration.

I don't mind a lot of walking, but the centre depresses me, on the whole; then the journey back seems to take forever. Still, I set off in that direction.

*

I noticed the lines marking the safety margin had been moved again, and had to take a detour.

'It's spreading,' I thought, though the jelly had stopped worrying me a long time ago. Meaning that I didn't say it sadly, as you might expect. It was just an observation.

As I drew nearer the centre I realised why I find it depressing, or at least one of the reasons. It's the women. Maybe because of the artificial light, they seem different somehow. From a distance, they almost all look like Llilli. I followed one, but she was much further ahead, and when she went into the churn-up I lost her; I'm sure it wasn't Llilli. That keeps on happening to me.

I didn't fancy the churn-up myself and peeled off down a side street. The sound of breaking glass ahead made me quicken my pace, but people were already dispersing, so I turned and walked away in frustration.

With my mind elsewhere, I made the foolish mistake of passing close to the fat ladies' meeting place, although, these days, you never know where they might find you. They all pounced on me like wild beasts and I was forced to run away; eventually I managed to shake them off, but I had to sacrifice a poor guy, caught unawares, who started to howl. I felt bad.

When I leant against a wall, to catch my breath, I was hit by a couple of sensations. First, I was hungry, and second, even though it had been the fat ladies, the chase had stirred my sexual desires. For a moment I had the crazy idea of doubling back and surrendering to the throng. I laughed. Annoyed, I realised there was nothing for it but to get hold of some money, unappealing as that was, so I gradually set myself in motion, to that end.

*

It was the middle of the night. I hadn't found anything. 'Of course,' I thought. 'It must get harder every day.' In the end

I steeled myself and went into the churn-up. You have to take more precautions in there, because it's not about who's the strongest or most agile; wherever you turn, people will stamp on you, crush you, leave you in bits.

It was a shame because a blonde girl had been following me for a while. 'She's not bad,' I thought, but my pockets were still empty and I soon lost sight of her; admittedly she might have had some money herself, and for a moment I considered the possibility, but I'm rather old-fashioned when it comes to all that. Damn pride, always getting in my way.

I managed to pick up a pretty full wallet. It was so easy I thought it might have been a trap, which is what happened to Ulises once. Luckily he escaped with the woman's handbag, but he barely made it out alive. I don't understand the twisted minds of people who lay traps. I suppose it's one of the idle distractions of the rich.

I left the churn-up and turned down a side street to get my bearings. The moon was out, but very faint. There's barely any street lighting away from the main avenue. I stowed the cash in my secret hiding place and tossed the wallet away. Carrying cash is such a nuisance. It leaves you vulnerable to anything. I've always thought some kind of barter system would be better.

*

I paid for the salami sandwich with a small note I'd kept separate and was clutching in my fist.

I haggled over the price to throw people off the scent. I didn't want them to realise I had money.

*

The prostitutes' street wasn't far away.

'Mister.'

'Mister.'

'Mister.'

'Mister.'

'Mister.'

'Mister.'

'Mister.'

I chose in a hurry because I didn't want to keep hearing that word. I'd have preferred someone younger. We agreed a price.

'The tunnel costs more,' she said, but I knew that already, and besides, it was still cheaper than the house, and had the advantage of being more private. 'Listen,' she said then, taking me by the arm and lowering her voice. 'You'd be better off paying up and leaving. You're going to get into trouble.'

'Why?' I asked.

'I'm a virgin,' she answered; I snorted with laughter. She got annoyed because I didn't believe her. It seemed crazy, she was thirty-five at least, perhaps forty. I laughed again.

'I warned you,' she said coldly, and I thought she seemed a little on edge.

*

We got down on all fours and began crawling into the tunnel. Our bodies brushed together and I made the most of this to grope her, though the angle was a bit awkward. Before going into the tunnel she'd rolled down her stockings, so as not to rip them. My knees hurt. I couldn't decide on a place; after a while she got tired and made me turn into a hollow on the right. There was a candle stub there and I lit it.

'Do we need to have light?' she asked, and I said yes. Reluctantly, she began to undress as I looked on.

'Well?' I asked, because she paused when she came to the final garments.

'You're rushing me,' she said, her voice hoarse.

While I reached into my clothes and took the money from the secret pocket in my underpants, she rather shyly finished undressing.

Her body wasn't anything special. Padding inside her clothes, everywhere. I caressed her all the same, but I felt I'd been swindled.

'Please,' she said. 'Don't hurt me.'

In all honesty, I'd have preferred to turn round and leave. I didn't see why I should spend money on that. The desire had vanished as if by magic. But I didn't dare offend her.

We looked at one another in silence. I thought she still seemed scared.

'What are you waiting for, mister?' she asked, at last; there was no insolence, or urgency, in her voice.

*

'Quick, your hand,' said the voice, and I felt the gun at my back and someone held the ink pad towards me. I couldn't argue. Claiming ignorance gets you nowhere, in the eyes of the law.

'I told you,' she said. 'You didn't listen.'

Her bloodstained garment was there, on a wooden stool, as legal evidence.

The gun prodded harder. Resentfully, I pressed my hand onto the ink pad. And then onto the paper. My whole hand. A green print. Then I was put through the wringer by that fat priest with the repulsive face.

'Do you, Miss Magenta Inés, take Mr . . .'

My name didn't matter. I declared myself to be Marco Tulio, which is what people call me – I think Hobbler came up with it, and I've never known why.

They even gave her a bouquet of flowers. White ones.

*

The bus was getting fuller and fuller and I felt dizzy, but for several reasons. Magenta pressed close to me, looking happy. I could have hit her. That dreamy expression. The ticket cost almost twice what she charges. I don't know how anyone travels these days.

The bus was carrying so much it could barely move. It's one every six hours, you have to bear in mind. We'd just about managed to sit down at the back, and that was when it began to fill up. Hands, legs, beach umbrellas, bags, buttocks, everything rubbing in our faces.

A placid-seeming woman in orange comfortably propped her crotch on my chin when I lifted my face to look at her. She smiled brazenly. It didn't feel right to move.

Then the fainting, passengers landing on top of us. When it was time to get off we were stuck, and went several stops too far. It was exhausting. I pushed and pushed, with Magenta making use of the space behind my body before it closed up again. People slid their hands into my pockets, but they didn't find the secret hiding place. As for Magenta, they squeezed at her padding, also quite calmly, and extracted her purse.

When the door opened in front of me, they took advantage of my momentum as I leapt off the bus, and deftly removed my jacket. They did the same with her coat and, though I have no idea how, her shoes.

*

Several days later. The early hours of the morning. A wildly erotic dream, about Llilli. Or perhaps it wasn't her, but I wanted it to be. When I woke up, someone was playing with my genitals; by the light of the match I saw it was the old couple's pesky little daughter. I slapped her away but she didn't cry; she was afraid of waking her parents. Since the match was lit, I decided to spark up a cigarette; there were grumbles.

I looked around for Magenta, but then remembered she was working, with the man who never takes his hat off. I don't know how she can stomach it, if only because of his hook nose and the bilious colour of his skin.

I got up to go to the bathroom; luckily, there was water. Afterwards I didn't want to go back to the room and started climbing the stairs instead. They wind around the edge of an iron structure, which is painted black and has a hole in the middle and things hanging inside it. I thought I'd never make it up; I was worn out and half asleep. My thoughts turned to Llilli.

*

As it happened, there was a space on the grass; I slept. On waking up, I saw the sun had come out, and the people in the park were laughing at the position of my hands.

*

I found myself unsure what to do next. I didn't feel like going anywhere. Then I realised I was hungry and bought a mortadella sandwich. I was missing the group by the fountain, but they wouldn't be meeting till the afternoon. I hadn't seen them, or anyone else. I wondered how the raid had gone. I still needed alcohol, more than before. Cigarettes

I could buy now I had some money, but alcohol is different, you have to get it in other ways. I doubted they'd have saved me any.

Then, although it's a bit far away, I decided to go to the port, since it was a cool morning and you could walk. I don't know what made me think of going to the port. I felt like it, for one thing, but I mean it had been ages since I last went, so I don't know why it occurred to me.

On a street in the old city I ran into the flock of mutants. Always a bad feeling. They move slowly, because some have to drag themselves along. Creatures made seemingly at random: one leg, three arms, eyes everywhere, edging forwards like beetles. The young teacher was in front, almost a girl. Green eyes. She looked at me for a little too long. I'd have liked to talk to her, but the mutants made me self-conscious, all those eyes watching me.

She seemed like a very nice girl. Such a shame. A song was coming from the flock, like a hymn; the singing wasn't bad. I couldn't make out the words, aside from something about cement.

*

Things were floating in the water and everything stank. 'Not the best day for the port,' I reflected. Some seagulls. The red horizon, clouds. 'Maybe it'll rain,' I said to myself, and thought of the water shortage, but what's disconcerting is that the two aren't really related. I've never known what affects whether there's water or not. If it did rain, I'd have gone out in it. I needed water, my whole body did.

I made my way along the breakwater and then the seafront. The beach was chock-a-block with people. I crossed over to the monument and found the young teacher under a palm tree.

'How can you stand them?' I asked, and she smiled and said you got used to it. 'They're adorable,' she added. I grimaced, then asked if she fancied a walk. She said she didn't have long but could give me a few minutes. We strolled together in silence and then I went with her to the colony; it's based in the semi-ruined cathedral.

I asked her name.

'The kids call me Ma.'

'I think I'll see you again, Ma,' I said, and waved goodbye in the doorway, moving three fingers of my right hand as if playing the piano.

As I walked away, the bells began to ring, and I quickened my pace. I wanted to get there and eat something, not because I didn't have any money but because I hadn't been for ages and, despite everything, I missed it.

*

Rumours spreading, murmurs in the crowd. They've stopped giving out spoons because people steal them. So how are we supposed to eat, by sticking our face in the bowl? Someone shows a yellow card and tries to push in;

the queue wasn't moving. I wasn't in a rush, sitting on the grass and gazing out over the wire fence. I could have gone back to sleep. I wondered if 'Ma' was short for 'maestra' – teacher – or 'mamá'. Whichever it was, I didn't want to call her that. She didn't look like Llilli, but I liked her. I don't know how else to explain it. I wished I knew her real name. People began going by with bowls of soup, the old men pouring most of it all over themselves. Some were indeed missing spoons. Discrimination, I thought. The queue had lost its shape and everyone was bunched together, jostling, fighting. They had to pause and order them all back in line. I don't know what the hurry was. There's enough to go round.

I stood up and decided to get in line myself, because the people who'd already eaten were now queueing up again, hoping to get another bowl.

*

There's a statue of a naked woman in the middle of the fountain. She's white all over and holding a jug. When times are good, the jug pours out a stream of water; now, however, it was dry. I tossed a load of money into the circle and everyone looked at me, astonished. After sharing it out they began asking questions, but I didn't want to give too many details. They hadn't gone on the raid because they'd been wondering where I was.

'You bunch of lazybones,' I said, and the word made

them laugh. I also gave them a couple of packs of cigarettes. 'I need alcohol,' I said. 'Today. Now.'

'Sllt,' said Ulises. He'd started that Joyce thing again; he knew it off by heart.

I told them about the teacher and they were disappointed. They'd been hoping for erotic details. But then Piggie's eyes lit up.

'I just remembered,' he said. 'There's a harpsichord. In the cathedral.'

Everyone was up for it. I made a sullen face.

'I barely know her,' I said, but in vain, because they were mobilising.

'And from there to the hospital,' they cried, full of enthusiasm; no, Worm said, the hospital first, but it was too early for that. Besides, I wouldn't take them if they were drunk. Even as it was, I had my doubts. I wasn't sure how much I could trust them.

*

Worm slithered and writhed, weeping. I was crouching down, my hands clasped to my neck. I think I was crying as well. It didn't matter that the harpsichord had seen better days. When silence fell, I requested the Chromatic Fantasia and Fugue. Piggie wiped his hands on his trousers and began. All of a sudden I saw the mutants begin to appear. I shut my eyes.

It was a while before I realised that Ma had slid alongside me. 'Be careful,' I whispered in her ear, pointing at my companions. They were all transported by the music, suffering horrendously. She nodded.

I don't know why she came. It made me nervous and distracted. When I noticed the music was about to finish I told her to go back inside and lock the doors, that I'd see her the next day. I kissed her hand.

*

The invalids managed to barricade themselves in, blocking the entrance with obstacles. In our effort to break down the door we snapped Hobbler's crutch, and he started swearing. Eventually the door gave way and we all burst in together; the invalids vanished. At the door to the lab we saw the doctor, his arms crossed.

'Get out of our way,' said Horacio, and the doctor shook his head. He was bald and wearing thick glasses.

'We don't want to hurt you,' said Hobbler, holding on to Dwarf so he didn't fall.

'We appreciate your work, doctor,' I said, 'and we have a little money. I hope we can come to an agreement.'

He shook his head, stubborn. I took a step closer and pushed him aside; he shoved me in the chest and sent me stumbling back.

Then we all surged forwards at once.

'Watch it!' shouted Worm, and we tried to dodge the punches on our way through.

'The invalids!' I heard the others shout, and when I turned

round, there they were, coming towards us, pushing gurneys and other blunt instruments on wheels. Skinny, in white pyjamas, they looked like ghosts, their faces gaunt.

We didn't want to cause any damage; they left us no choice. A lot of things got broken and one invalid came off pretty badly. I seized a three-gallon demijohn, but Piggie told me to smell it first in case they'd mixed it with eucalyptus oil. When it was all over, we regrouped by the fountain.

*

'Llilli!' I shouted, and began staggering after her. The white scarf around her head, the shape of her legs, the little leather boots, black with white fur trim. But it wasn't her, and when I turned the corner I tumbled into the fat ladies' arms. There was no way out. They almost ripped me to shreds, fighting among themselves, and I started to vomit.

They took me to a house and attempted to revive me with coffee. I came round a bit but pretended to be more drunk, trying to find a way out. But I couldn't.

They tore off my clothes, and their own, and fell upon me, fighting all the while. Those horrible bodies; I vomited again but by now there was nothing left in my stomach.

*

I woke up in the ruins. Fortunately I had my clothes on, but all my money was gone. I saw the sun was high in the sky. My head ached, my tongue was swollen, my stomach was on fire. When I sat up I felt a terrible pain in my testicles.

I gripped the walls, swaying, struggling to see in the sun. I imagined my eyes were completely bloodshot; I couldn't open them properly and everything looked red. I lay back down in the shade, my throat parched.

'Water,' I said, but I couldn't move. When I woke up, it was raining.

*

I didn't fancy the circle, and I was in no state to see Ma. So I went to the room and lay down on the floor. Magenta didn't ask any questions. She brought something to eat and I nibbled a little, and asked for some water. When night fell people started arriving and they woke me up, inconsiderately. I yelled at them to be quiet, but they took no notice. After all the whooping and hallooing I'd done in my time, they said. At ten the light was turned out. The Italian woman moaned softly, and I covered my head with the pillow. Magenta bit my shoulder and I told her to get lost; she knows I'm attracted to the Italian woman and get jealous when she and her husband make love, which is almost every night.

I asked Magenta for some more water. My throat was dry. She says that by the time she came back I was asleep.

*

Several days later.

'I didn't think I'd see you again,' said Ma, and I heard the gentle reproach in her voice.

'Something came up,' I replied, without explaining anything, not even that I'd walked past the palm tree by the monument the day before, thinking I'd see her, though I couldn't bring myself to go to the cathedral.

She noticed my bad mood. We walked along.

'I need to be alone, with you,' I said. 'There's nowhere. Not the tunnel, not the cathedral, somewhere clean, empty, maybe the ruins, but that's too dangerous, and I'd like there to be grass, and trees, and I'd like to be clean as well, not even I can stand myself being so sweaty, if only everything were different, you know?'

She smiled, squeezed my hand, said that none of that mattered. We went to the ruins. The sky looked ominous. It was the afternoon, but there wasn't much light. I lay down in the rubble, and she rested her head on my stomach and asked me to recite something.

'I don't know,' I said; she insisted, I got muddled halfway through a Neruda poem and refused to carry on. Then she recited in French, as if she were having a conversation, something very soft and very sad, I didn't catch more than the odd word or phrase, it reminded me of the Yves Montand version of a Prévert poem, 'Barbara', the same rainy atmosphere, or maybe it was the way she recited it. I stroked her breasts through her dress, we kissed, she didn't stir any desire in me, it was different, something new, I wanted to stroke her hair and she made me think of jelly or sea voyages. I felt very old and weary.

She said maybe I didn't want her and that was why I was so distant, and I said it wasn't that, but I couldn't explain because I didn't know myself, and it would be better if we didn't speak.

'Tell me we'll never be parted,' she said.

'Never,' I answered, and then threw myself on top of her, pushing her into a corner, pressing her flat against the uneven ground; the lame people were passing by, searching, clattering with their crutches. I felt genuine terror. Ma didn't realise what was happening. I covered her mouth with my hand.

The dark sky was on our side, and they passed close by without seeing us. Ma tried to struggle free; I did my best to convey my distress to her through my body. They searched, clattered, tripped on clods of earth and swore, I glimpsed a scrap of black cloth and the wood of a crutch.

'It's over,' I said then, and on the way back she huddled very close to me. Now she was afraid.

*

Horacio's report was very long and full of technical jargon. I got bored.

'... which gives rise,' he concluded, standing on the rock, in glasses and a dark overcoat, 'to the inevitable conclusion that, given that the substance of the jelly is indestructible (non-fragmentable and therefore non-edible), we must abandon this proposal and instead wait, resigned, until sooner or later it devours us, within a predicted time frame (allowing, of course, for the difficulty of making such estimates) of between one and ten years.'

Someone clapped, someone else made a rude noise with their mouth. I turned down the maté because my stomach was still in a bad way.

I took Horacio aside and talked to him about Llilli. He said it seemed like an insoluble problem, which could only, as a last resort, be solved by leaving it to chance, but that nonetheless, he needed to know all the details before coming to a definite conclusion.

'No, no,' he said, when I started describing her: the very dark hair, the brown eyes, the little fur-trimmed boots, the perfect legs. 'No, no; I'm not about to go looking for her, MT. I mean the meeting place, details like that.'

'It was in the churn-up,' I said, and I saw him shake his head sadly, hopelessly. 'Then I mentioned the tunnel, but she said not the tunnel, and I thought she was right, and I said not the room either, there are too many people, and she didn't offer another solution. I don't have any money, I said, and she told me to try and find some and that in the meantime she'd wait for me somewhere. I asked where, and had the feeling she wanted to get rid of me; but I wasn't about to let her slip through my fingers, and she said how about the patisserie, it's safe there. I don't like the patisserie because it's where the elegant men go, and for all I knew she'd be seduced by a suit or a Brylcreemed side-parting, but I had no other choice so in she went and sat down and smiled at me through the window. I set off in torment, convinced I was losing her, and I don't know if I'm boring you with these details but that's all of it, Horacio, I don't have anything more concrete, it took me a while to get back and when I did she was gone, I flung the money down on the pavement, which set off a great brawl in the churn-up, people killing each other, I broke the window with my fists and got covered in cuts.'

'Did you go back to the patisserie?' Horacio asked. His eyes were narrowed; he was thinking. He's a thinking machine.

'Every day. I used to shower and shave at the Baths Club. I even bought myself a suit, but she never showed up.'

'Anything from the conversation?'

'She talked a lot, but there was nothing specific; she said she didn't like the churn-up, and only went that time out of boredom.'

'The bus?'

'She didn't mention it.'

'Language?'

'Educated.'

'Right.' He scratched his head. 'It sounds like she's a nice girl, probably from the wooded area. Have you tried there?'

'Every day, every night, my hands in my pockets, howling at the moon.'

'You could try again,' he said, without much enthusiasm. 'It's tough. A needle in a haystack, of course. I'd keep trying the wooded area, and the patisserie.'

'I can't go back to that, Horacio,' I said, shaking my head. 'I can't think about a suit again, or about the Baths.'

'Prejudice?' He smiled sardonically. 'Why a suit?' He scratched his nose with his thumb.

*

I went to the churn-up. Not to look for Llilli – Horacio had dissuaded me – but to take the edge off my depression. I'd found that if I didn't move my legs the crowd still carried me along, and sometimes the crush, the stamping, the groping, gave me a masochistic pleasure, and there was something thrilling about the risk of falling, just like that, with my hands in my pockets. At one point I was pushed into a window, but it didn't break; I just bumped my head slightly, then the crowd dragged me on.

A long stretch with my nose stuck in an old lady's fur hat, it smelt of mothballs, I breathed in with gusto and got quite drunk, then my head started to hurt. After that I managed to wedge myself against the body of a tall, robust woman of a certain age, resting my chin on her spine, which she seemed to enjoy. A prematurely bald guy with glasses and a funny pointed beard kept trying to walk in the opposite direction to the churn-up, and ended up going backwards. I stuck my tongue out at him. Then I slipped in between two women and put my arms around their shoulders and hung there, bending my knees. At first they laughed but then they got tired and almost dropped me.

I left the pavement and made my way along the soft tarmac. My shoes kept sticking and it was hard to make progress. People didn't understand and kept pointing and laughing. I walked among the piles of old wrecks sinking gradually into the tarmac, once automobiles, now immobile. Eventually I managed to tire myself out and went to get some sleep.

*

'Leave your gloves by the river,' I said to Llilli, and offered her a piece of dark chocolate; then I realised I was dreaming and that's when I should have woken up; I tried not to, but the dream changed regardless and along came the spiders and false teeth. More and more people in the room, I don't know who's letting them in; I can't complain, no one really objected when I brought Magenta, but this is too many, the bodies are almost touching, I can't lie crossways and I have to sleep stiffly, without moving, then I wake up exhausted and don't feel like doing anything.

Magenta stirred at my side. She wasn't working because it was a Friday and I found myself obliged to have relations with her. I don't enjoy it, but I suppose it's part of my duties as a married man, and at any rate she was left unsatisfied.

I sat up slightly and lit a cigarette, then came the nausea and that itch in my pyloric valve. The chorus of breathing, in some cases asthmatic, and the snores started to get to me and before long I was struggling to breathe myself. I coughed, but decided I'd better not spit, since there wouldn't be any space. I got up and went to the bathroom; despite my best efforts I ended up treading on part of a person, and was furiously sworn at. I didn't feel like going back after that. I attempted to sleep on the tiles in the courtyard, but I soon felt that stabbing pain in my shoulder blade and began to fear for my lungs.

I returned to the room, trod on someone again, got sworn at again, then there were mutterings and an argument spread, which I kept out of. I lit a match to see who was on my right – Magenta was on my left – hoping it would be the Italian woman, but it was the toothless old man, who squinted at me out of the corner of his eye and asked if I ever slept. I didn't answer and tried to drift off; I felt lethargic, full of indecipherable desires.

I couldn't think about Llilli so in the end I thought about Ma, about where I could take her the next day, and then I thought that what we had couldn't last, the whole thing was somehow absurd, it was all her fault, I don't know what she saw in me, but I was pursuing her, and for what? There weren't many places to choose from, the ruins, I couldn't take her to the fountain because sooner or later she'd be raped; I wouldn't be surprised if those guys had even raped the statue. Worm used to kiss its breasts and caress its buttocks.

Somewhere green, trees, grass, deserted. Magenta had noticed I was awake and started to nag me. I said something rude and turned my back. She'd interrupted my train of thought. Just at that moment I'd had an inkling of a place, it had formed in my mind less as a presence than an absence, a kind of yearning, but I knew it was there in my memory, and that it was real, not just a yearning, maybe something from my childhood, some out-of-reach or perhaps now non-existent place, or a distorted recollection, perhaps of a tall bush, or a plot of tomato plants. I fell asleep.

*

'We need to get out of here, it's unbearable,' Magenta said the next day.

'Agreed,' I replied.

*

'You could come to the cathedral,' said Ma. 'The ruins are busy, full of people, but there's a room that even has a key, and no one uses it for fear it might collapse. It could be dangerous, I think, in a strong wind, but maybe it would work for you, at least for a while, or you could devise some kind of protection.'

'Fine by me,' I said. 'I'd like to move in right away.'

'Do you have much stuff?' she asked.

'Nothing.'

*

Ma got hold of various sacks, and we lay on some and covered ourselves with the others. She was clearly waiting for me to make a move. But I felt good like that, alone with her, until suddenly I realised that even she was annoying me, and that I wanted to be alone, completely alone, locked inside the room. 'What's wrong with me?' I thought. 'Am I so old that even this girl's getting on my nerves?'

I noticed she'd embarked on some complicated manoeuvres, and her face was flushed. I took the sack-blankets by one corner and lifted them up. She'd undressed. 'Fine, fine,' I said to her. 'I'll show you I'm not as dead as you thought.'

She wasn't a virgin, she knew how to make love, but it still made me hate myself. I'd never thought about her like that. I don't know if she picked up on my concern, a certain lack of spontaneity. I felt everything had been spoilt, that the rot had set in. 'The process is speeding up,' I said to myself, and spent the rest of the day inside the room, not eating, deep in thought. At one point the door handle moved. It must have been Ma but I didn't want to open it; I wanted her to think I'd gone out. That night I slept very well. The floor was hard and cold but the sacks did a good job, and

I could thrash around to my heart's content: I woke up free of sacks, on the other side of the room.

*

Several days later. The solitude had done me good. Ma stared at me open-mouthed when I handed her the roll of sacks.

'It's hopeless,' I told her. 'I don't want to abuse your hospitality. I don't love you. I don't want to sleep with you. I like the way you recite in French, I love you as a sister, but I find all this disgusting, not you, but me, like incest or something, it's just not working.'

It was the afternoon, she started crying, I stroked her hair and then went to the circle by the fountain. I sat on the rock and they said I'd lost weight, and was it love or hunger.

'I've remembered one detail,' I said, aside, to Horacio. 'She talked a lot about Pergolesi.'

He clapped a hand to his forehead and began to grin so delightedly it seemed cruel. I was afraid he might say 'Eureka'.

'Pull yourself together,' I told him, because he was stammering. He said he was absolutely certain she must be one of the trauma victims at the City, that establishment where educated people meet up and get drunk in secret. A famous café, but under the counter, apparently, they even serve methylated spirits.

'Do you think so?' I asked, sticking out my lower lip (to show disappointment).

'Definitely,' he said.

*

I couldn't believe it, my own bad luck, always, invariably. Something had stopped me finding the City until then, and now, of course, there were the red lines. Still, I went inside, very carefully, because sometimes the jelly is almost invisible, but I wasn't expecting any nice surprises.

The jelly had covered exactly half of the café; the other half, needless to say, was deserted.

I wandered among the evacuated blocks, and it felt so strange to see the empty streets, houses, whole flats, all completely uninhabited, not a soul in sight. 'Such a waste,' I thought, quickening my pace, because the jelly could grow at any moment. But then someone called out to me from one corner, precisely level with a red line.

Ruth, beloved fat old Ruth, leaning out of a ground-floor window.

'Silly old hag,' I said, and kissed her on the cheek. Then, resting my hands on the windowsill, I looked suspiciously at the jelly. 'You could have asked for some cyanide. It would be more pleasant.'

'Come on in,' she said. 'Or are you afraid?'

'I'm very afraid,' I replied, but I went in all the same. A magnificent apartment.

'One of my discoveries,' she said, proudly. 'They paint the lines with a safety margin, and they're always over-cautious. When everyone's evicted, I move in. It's different every time, a change of scene. They leave and I arrive. Would you like a Coca-Cola from the fridge-freezer?'

'Nerves of steel,' I told her. 'The growth is predictable, to an extent; one day you'll wake up and there'll be no more Ruth. You should've listened to Horacio, and his report about . . .' I trailed off. 'Only a stupid old woman . . .'

'That's just it,' she said. 'I might be old, but I'm not stupid. I want to spend the time I have left living like what I really am, a queen. All my life I've been covered in fleas and just once I wanted things to be different. Now it's two baths a day and central heating. Fancy listening to some records? Charles Aznavour in Spanish, Cafrune, a whole record shop's worth, all LPs. Long players.'

She tried again with the Coca-Cola, but I asked for alcohol instead.

'Alcohol!' she said. 'You lout! There's Scotch, the real stuff. But let me show you the fridge-freezer. There's a little light inside.'

I didn't want to disappoint her.

'And not a word to anyone,' she said. 'Otherwise, even though there are thousands of buildings in this position, there won't be any space left for me.'

'Don't you worry,' I said, tasting the whisky, but I didn't like it; maybe my palate had got used to the pure stuff;

I positively preferred neutral alcohol these days. But I didn't say anything. Ruth was very happy, and I was happy to see her happy.

'Are you staying the night?' she asked. 'There's a whole guest room, it's amazing. Tiles in the bathroom, a bidet.'

'Hot water?' I asked.

'Naturally. And a bath.'

I forgot all about the jelly. I had to drain the first lot of water almost immediately and then refill the bath, that's how filthy I was.

'You're so thin,' said Ruth. She came in and looked at me floating there. I'd filled my lungs and risen to the surface, then let out the air and was sinking under again. I asked her to leave because it was embarrassing to be watched. She came back in an hour and found me asleep.

'You'll drown or die of pneumonia or other causes,' she said. 'It's not good to stay in for so long.'

I lay down, still slightly damp, in an enormous double bed.

'Shall I turn on the heating?' she asked.

'Good God no,' I replied, and we said good night, and then, as she put it, she retired to her rooms.

*

When I stepped outside the next day, I almost dropped dead from cardiac arrest on seeing the jelly some eight inches from my nose. The red lines must have been moved several blocks, because I couldn't see them any more.

'Crazy old witch!' I shouted in through the window. She was still in bed and I saw her stomach quivering with laughter. 'Can't you see where the jelly is? We escaped by the skin of our teeth – don't tempt me again with your unbridled luxury.'

She carried on laughing and waved goodbye, after removing her hand from between the sheets. I shrugged and went to see Anselmo.

*

That afternoon.

Horacio asked me how I'd got on, and I told him the jelly had swallowed the City. He couldn't say where the people had moved on to. Perhaps they'd all dispersed.

'It'll be harder for you now,' he said, stroking his chin. 'Pity.'

*

'We should take action,' I said, and sucked on the maté straw. Everyone was looking at me. I was always worried about something, though my ideas never went anywhere.

'What kind of action?' asked Piggie, not catching my drift.

'Oh, I don't know,' I said, with a vague gesture. 'Something with the jelly, the blind people, the city, this isn't working, can't you see? We're getting older, I said to Anselmo today. Of course, he didn't understand. He's got his hole, but what about us?'

The maté ran out and I handed the gourd back to Hobbler, who was listening closely. I nodded at him to say thanks.

'In practical terms . . .' said Ulises.

'In practical terms, nothing,' I said. 'It's just a feeling. I can't explain it. Something we need more of, or less of, I don't know.'

'I think I get you,' said Piggie. 'It must be like a harpsichord. There are days when you feel like playing, but not always, and other days when the same thing needs expressing in a different way. Socially, for example, by taking the blind out for lunch, or working out how to destroy the jelly.'

I made a strange movement with my head, as if to say that was it but not exactly.

Dwarf. I knew he was going to open his mouth and say her name. The man must be obsessed.

'Like searching for Llilli,' said Dwarf. 'A mass operation, involving all of us.'

I went to the room feeling something unfathomable. An urge not to go to bed. To take action.

*

Magenta never complains to me, but this time, she said, I'd gone too far, people were talking, there had even been a proposal from one man, a manager by profession.

'Deaf ears,' I retorted, and went to bed with a thuggish expression, glaring defiantly at them all.

*

There really were more people now. I couldn't bear it, not after the cathedral, or Ruth, or the solitude; the contact with other bodies was unavoidable, someone using my calves as a pillow. Magenta and I both on our sides, no space to lie on our backs. Intolerable, by now, the mix of smells.

'Get your things, we're going,' I said to Magenta. It must have been three in the morning, I hadn't slept a wink.

'Where?' she asked.

'I don't know,' I said. 'Not here. No more. I've had enough.'

*

'The tunnel?' she suggested; I shook my head. It's a long way away, I'd rather not sleep, even just for one night, and it's so stuffy. It's not the answer.

'Where did you use to sleep, before?'

'With the girls,' she replied. 'In shifts, which kept changing, so annoying.'

I probed a bit more but I could see she didn't want to go back to that. There was the cathedral, though that would upset Ma, I didn't know how I'd explain it to her. Ruth's solution? I didn't have the guts. If I were really old, perhaps, but probably not even then.

We leant on the shop's wooden shutters, supporting one another as we dozed standing up, fitfully, never deeply.

*

Later, we argued. Bitterly. In the end, I calmed down and said, to put an end to things:

'You go your way and I'll go mine. I'll settle somewhere, I don't know where, and so will you. The problem is both of us together. Maybe one day we'll meet again. For now, goodbye.'

I turned and walked away, relieved. I felt sure things would improve after this. With Llilli it would be different, I knew I'd be able to rack my brains and come up with a solution, but Magenta didn't inspire me, it wasn't worth my while. 'What do you know about Pergolesi?' I wanted to ask, but why torture her? It was better this way.

*

I lay on my belly and then, lowering my head a little way into the hole, shouted:

'Need any labourers?'

A head popped up, but it was a young man, not Anselmo. Then Anselmo appeared as well.

'I've hired a labourer,' he said. 'His name's Luís.'

'Pleased to meet you, Luís,' I said, but we couldn't shake hands because he needed both of his to hold on to the edge of the hole.

'Still, you know, there's always something for you,' said Anselmo, and I realised he wasn't telling the truth. He didn't need me for anything, and I've never been much use to him.

'No, thanks, I was just joking,' I said with a smile, and sat up.

As I walked away, I turned and shouted over my shoulder: 'How's it all going?'

'Oh, you know,' he called after me, and I saw the heads disappear.

*

One week later, or thereabouts.

Tired, night and day, of the park, I decided to leave and that afternoon I went to the circle, with no real sense of what I'd do later on when it was time to find somewhere to spend the night. I was in despair. That pile of naked corpses. I couldn't believe it.

Something grabbed at my feet and then pulled itself up by my trousers. Worm.

'You see,' he said, weeping.

'The only one?' I asked, and he said yes.

'Hobbler?

'Piggie?

'Ulises?'

His response, somewhere between nodding and shaking his head, always the same.

'Horacio?

'Dwarf?'

(A longer pause.)

'And you?'

'I was by the fountain, never mind what I was doing, the point is they didn't see me, but that makes no difference, I had to suffer through the whole thing, the lame people turned up, they've always hated us and there were more of them than ever, hundreds, our lot defended themselves like lions, like ferocious tigers, real beasts, but they were outnumbered, and you see, I couldn't do anything, I'm a coward, it was hopeless. Dwarf caused a bloodbath, as for Horacio, I never thought he'd put up such a fight, and Hobbler, everyone, but it was hopeless, they took everything, they even stripped their own fallen comrades.'

They hadn't broken the fountain but now it had no meaning, a marble goddess, the empty jug. Hobbler, Dwarf, Ulises, Piggie, Horacio.

'And Ruth?' I asked.

'She hasn't come by for ages. Luckily she was spared, though maybe she's long dead. We never saw her again.'

*

'MT!' Worm yelled when he saw me walking away, but I didn't turn back. I was fond of Worm, but he would only have clung to me, and then how to get rid of him, day in, day out.

'Marco!' he yelled, but I didn't turn back.

*

I tried to follow a logical route in my search, but there are thousands of buildings and I had no way of knowing, in my exhaustion, if Ruth had been swallowed by the jelly or moved further out. I knocked on door after door, shouted her name through window after window, and repeated my search the next day, to no avail.

'This is a situation,' I thought, 'in which nothing can be known for sure.'

*

No, I can't handle the park, in summer perhaps, but it's so cold at night these days, and it's only getting worse, what's awful is the dew, or the frost, you wake up frozen stiff in the early morning, the air burns like fire when it hits your nostrils, you get sick, your clothes soaked through, as if you'd had a bucket of water tipped all over you, and the coughing. Some people can put up with it, but not me. I'm not used to it.

*

The room was packed. I knew it. Some people had left, but I couldn't count properly because it was so crowded. There was the guy with the hat, asleep. I couldn't see the Italian woman, but her husband was in a corner. She must have been somewhere around, or maybe she'd gone. There was no space for me, at any rate, though I was sure others would move in. Still, it's not for me. I'm very delicate. This many people get on my nerves. I can't sleep on top of other bodies, or sitting up. And the smell.

*

My sleep pattern changed. I slept during the day, in the ruins, and at night I wandered around, freezing cold, not eating properly. I managed to find an overcoat, but the cold was coming from within.

*

No doubt Ma thought it was because of the room, and maybe she was right, but I told myself I needed to see her. I was pursuing her again, without quite knowing why. There was a new teacher helping her out, she said, a young man, they were an item now, that was fine by me. She said I could share the room with him, but I assured her there was no need. I'd just wanted to say hello, and I was pleased to see her happy.

A mutant sidled up, realised who I was and tried to climb me, pouting his lips.

'The kids remember,' said Ma. 'They ask after you sometimes. Now, don't be mean. Can't you see he wants to give you a kiss?'

I offered my cheek instead, but I wasn't disgusted. I even felt quite affectionate, you could almost call the kid beautiful, though why so many eyes? The new teacher came over and looked at me curiously. I said hello.

I'd have liked Ma to recite something in French, but it wouldn't have fit the mood. An inopportune moment.

'Right, anyway,' I said, and pretended to look at my watch, though Ma would be fairly sure I didn't have one.

'I'm pleased to see you looking so well, and we'll have the chance to talk more another time.'

*

I got up just in time to reach the port and watch the sunset. A few days ago I'd discovered it was well worth seeing: the purple oval, fragmented by wisps of cloud, expanding above the red sky, after which it's swallowed by the sea and everything turns purple for a moment. Then the night.

I went to the churn-up and felt nothing. I picked up a beautiful wallet but there wasn't much money in it. As I walked over the tarmac, I thought about standing still and letting myself sink, but it would take a long time, I'd only get bored, and besides, it might not make it above my ankles.

As always when I passed the patisserie, I looked inside, with the usual hope, almost a reflex action.

Llilli.

She was laughing, sitting at a table with several people around her, so elegant with her defiant profile, her black hair now in a plait, her deep, shining eyes, her hands.

I went in, sat down at a nearby table and looked at her, she glanced my way a couple of times but didn't seem to recognise me, a waiter came, I ordered a tea, he made a strange face, because of my clothes, of course.

Adorable Llilli, I hadn't embellished her in her absence; the sight of her was better than the very best memory. Eventually she sensed my insistent gaze and waved to me, smiling, then they all got up to leave, men and women, I stood up too, touched her shoulder, said 'You remember me,' and she said 'Yes, Marco Tulio,' and laughed, maybe at me, I don't know, then I said 'I want to see you,' and she said 'Not now,' and I said 'When?' and she said 'Tomorrow morning at eight, here,' and they all went into the churn-up. I paid for the tea I hadn't touched and then went into the churn-up as well.

*

Eight o'clock, nine, ten, eleven, twelve, I'd dressed up as a gentleman, I drank gallons of tea, the waiter kept looking at me, Llilli didn't turn up, I knew it.

*

I sank into the bath and dozed off. Some time later, I awoke and climbed into the big bed to sleep.

I composed a prayer to the jelly: holy mother, shelter us in your lap. Then I thought about Ruth, and Hobbler, and Piggie, and Horacio, and Dwarf, and Ulises, and Worm and Magenta, and Ma, and the mutant who kissed me, and myself.

'Llilli,' I thought.

*

The next morning.

I opened the window, pulled the cord to raise the blind, and a kind of transparent mass began to ooze, very gradually, into the room; it seemed to be growing, and had air bubbles here and there, and reminded me of honey, only more solid, like flesh. I tried to shut the window but it was impossible. Nothing could hold the thing back.

I dressed as fast as I could, feeling ridiculous in my suit, and gingerly opened the door of the flat; there was no jelly in sight; I set off down the stairs towards the ground floor, but the jelly had made it in through the main entrance and was climbing the stairs, slowly, inexorably, like boiling milk; I spun around and retraced my steps.

The jelly seeping in through the window of the room where I slept wasn't yet seeping out through the door of the flat; I carried on up to the second floor and tried the doors, but they were locked; it was the same on the third floor, and the fourth.

On the fifth I found one that was open; I hurried through it, shut it behind me, looked out of the windows that faced the street and there it was, pressing against the glass, you could barely see the pavement.

I was seized by claustrophobia, knowing that even if the windows held, I would die in the end, a drawn-out death, from suffocation, or hunger, or thirst, and I didn't want that, but nor did I have the courage to go into the jelly. Perhaps last night I could have done it, but not now.

I moved through the house, inspecting all the windows. At the back there was a service bathroom, and its narrow little window was jelly-free.

Five floors. Below, an empty courtyard.

I pulled my body through the little window, trying to stay calm and not look down (to avoid vertigo).

Gripping hold of a drainpipe, I found a couple of footholds, I don't know how, it was as if I were clinging to the wall with my fingernails. I began to sweat and my back prickled, my face prickled and most of all my nose, my whole head. I was convinced I wouldn't make it out alive. In the end, my survival instinct prevailed; time after time I wanted to let go and be done with it, but my hands held on of their own accord, and my feet balanced of their own accord on ledges and windowsills; all my muscles were aching and every so often I started to tremble, and my heart danced in my chest and leapt as high as my throat. After one sudden slip my foot steadied itself but then I was frozen like that for an hour, or several hours, or who knows how long, unable to move; then I carried on, and it happened again, and at last I decided to let go for real, I couldn't take it any more, I looked down thinking I'd still be at the fourth floor, or the third, and ended up shaking with laughter when I saw that my feet were practically brushing the courtyard.

*

I walked through the house. Moving was difficult, everything hurt, but I had to get out of there.

*

It was the priest, now in civilian dress. He looked less unpleasant than he had as a priest. I could see Magenta too, and some others. I was in the ruins.

'What do you lot want?' I asked rudely.

The priest took out some written papers.

'Proceedings in the name of Magenta Inés against Marco Tulio. Desertion. Corporal punishment.'

I tried to escape, but it was impossible; they caught me in no time. Then a brutal beating that left me naked and bruised. I thought I might have broken a bone or two, and I couldn't see straight.

*

'In search of new horizons,' I said to Worm. He'd stayed loyal, though I don't know how he could bear the stench of the corpses. The fountain was broken (the statue cracked).

'Now no more water will pour from the jug,' he said, and I thought he'd lost his mind.

June 1967
Tr. AM

THE GOLDEN REFLECTIONS

I slipped into my coat, checked the neatness of my appearance in the mirror (my hairstyle, in particular), and made my way down the hall towards the front door. When I looked at my watch, I saw I still had fifteen minutes to get to the office; I could take my time and enjoy the pleasant autumn air, since the route there from my house could be covered in four or five minutes on foot. It was then, just as my hand was about to touch the door handle, that I heard the unusual sound.

(A sound as if from a ping-pong ball, a bit larger than the typical kind, bouncing rhythmically – don't think of the noise of the celluloid striking the tile, but imagine the pure sound directly after impact, and its echoes – or a wooden hammer, wrapped in cloth, knocking on a thick iron pipe. The rhythm was consistent; the sounds were about a second apart, and all of equal force.)

My hand stopped before reaching the door handle and, automatically, I turned to look towards the space behind the cupboard in the corner of the living room. I set off in that direction, but as I was walking I became increasingly convinced that the sound wasn't coming from there after all. I got down on my hands and knees and looked under the cupboard; in the corner there was nothing but dust, and now the sound was further away.

As I made my way back to the door, the illusion that the sound was coming from behind the cupboard returned. I retraced my steps and stood next to the cupboard, and from there I thought I'd pinpointed it inside the telephone table; I hurried over and opened the little door, but found nothing but the phone book and a pencil, and now I had the impression that the sound was coming from the bathroom.

The origin of the sound, I told myself then, must almost certainly be outside. As happens with crickets and the squeaking of rats, an acoustic mirage was making it seem like it was coming from indoors. Out I went.

I walked around the (admittedly rather unkempt) garden in its entirety, including the gravel surrounding it – a narrow border – listening carefully all the while. Then I manoeuvred along the garden walls, peering at the neighbours' houses, but there was no trace of the sound.

Back inside, even before closing the door behind me, I could clearly hear the rhythm, which had, it seemed, continued uninterrupted during my brief absence.

After checking all the rooms, I felt sure it must be coming from the attic.

I'd forgotten about the attic ages ago. As a child I used to spend my time up there playing with the piles of junk, especially the contents of two or three trunks. Now, as I picked my way up the creaky stairs, the banister wobbling alarmingly, a slight blush spread over my cheeks when I recalled the mannequin. It more or less faithfully represented a woman's form, except for the head – which it didn't have – and the legs, which had been replaced with a solid wooden stand. I remembered how unnerving the mannequin had seemed when I was four or five, and the mysterious smell, which I had found particularly exciting, and remembered that the idea of sex, around that time, had begun to pique my interest.

Getting into the attic was no small task, since the door was swollen; a strong musty smell hit me as soon as I got it open. I checked my watch: five minutes had passed. I still had time.

I flicked the light switch but it didn't turn on; then I realised the bulb it controlled was missing. I had to open the window, after feeling my way across the attic between heaps of stuff in the dark. I got a blast of fresh air and a curious, revitalised view of the neighbourhood as a whole. There was more greenery in the surrounding area than I'd realised; the roofs of the houses were a beautiful red, and only much further off could I see the filthy grey hodgepodge of buildings in the centre.

I had a look at the mannequin and smiled when I found it didn't turn me on in the slightest. Nor was its smell anything like the one I'd whiffed in my childhood. Maybe, I thought, the damp had changed it, or perhaps the years had affected my sense of smell, or the corresponding associations. And the general appearance of the thing was unfortunate, a satirical caricature of a fat, haughty old woman.

There were piles of wood; antique blinds; a painter's easel I couldn't remember ever seeing before; wrought-iron headboards adorned with laborious reliefs of flowers and leaves; a big run-down mercury mirror, which momentarily reflected my face, making it look consumed by leprosy; and the trunks.

I couldn't resist opening one of them. It didn't have a lock. Inside was a depressing collection of old, grungy fabrics, in which I no longer recognised the fabulous treasures from my youth. I didn't bother opening the others.

Then I went back to the window for a breath of fresh air and to take in the beautiful new view of the houses and trees.

The church clock struck two. At first, I accepted the sound as just another pleasing, logical brushstroke, a detail of the landscape; but then I realised with a start that, for the first time in two years, I was going to be late to the office.

As soon as I shut the attic door (I'd left the window open, to air out the space), and before my foot landed on the first stair, I heard once again – and remembered, since I'd completely forgotten about it up there – the sound that had sent me looking all over the house. Nothing about it had changed, and now, not only by process of elimination this time, I understood that it was coming from the basement.

(The entrance to the basement is under the stairs to the attic; it's not a door, strictly speaking, but rather an opening covered with a curtain; a sort of trap for anyone who doesn't know about the stairs hidden behind it. Ever since I'd ended up alone in the house, I'd never thought to go down there.)

As I left the attic, I thought to myself that I'd be better off forgetting the sound; it was unacceptable to my pride and my sense of duty to be late to the office and, what's more, to almost certainly get an earful from my boss. Our relationship wasn't entirely positive, even though I did my work perfectly and he recognised this. It was more a question of personal incompatibility, perhaps a problem of clashing star signs.

But as I walked past the curtain, the sound became clearer and more powerful; this time, there could be no doubt whatsoever about where it was coming from, and my curiosity – or perhaps, though I'm not trying to justify myself, a sense of duty even deeper than the one that binds me to my office – became impossible to resist. I went into the kitchen and picked up the box of matches. I lit one, shielding it with my left hand, then stepped through the opening, moving the curtain aside with my shoulder, and started to walk down the stairs.

I was forced to use up another couple of matches, in part because I had to make my way down extremely slowly, since the concrete steps were narrow and their edges dangerously sharp, and also because a sudden draught blew out the flames, despite the protection of my hand and the lack of windows in the basement.

I went on lighting matches over the course of my search. All I found were piles of demijohns, and baskets full of demijohns, and pipes running across the ceiling just above my head.

But the sound wasn't coming from the pipes, either. I touched each one with my fingers and felt no vibration at all. Then I knocked on them, first with my fist, and then with the heel of one of my shoes, and the sound they made was nothing like the sound in question, which remained as constant and rhythmical as ever.

Suddenly, the same draught pricked my right eye, like a needle; I wasn't holding a match in my fingers at the time, and I made out a tiny speck of light ahead. It was, beyond any doubt and despite the impossibility, a ray of sunshine.

I walked towards it and it disappeared; I stepped back, trying to return to my original position, and moved my head around slowly, in an attempt to find it. At the same time, I felt at the breast pocket of my jacket, took my glasses from their case and put them on, afraid the draught might prick my eye again.

At last I located the ray of light, held out my right hand at eye level, palm flat, and then, peering out from under it all the while, moved very slowly forwards. In this way, I was able to locate the tiny hole in the wall. I put my eye up to it.

The scene couldn't possibly have been real. And yet there it was.

A place somewhere between a park and a forest, which immediately brought to mind certain Botticelli paintings: the light was spring-like and crisp, the variety of greens infinite, and everything, the trees, the plants, the people – because there were people too – shimmered with golden reflections.

A man in a check shirt and wide-brimmed hat was drinking from a bottle, spilling the contents all over his shirt; a girl with long blonde hair was walking naked through the trees with a bird on her shoulder; another girl, with wavy black hair, was eating an apple; blue-eyed children were playing in silence, sitting in a circle on the ground and smiling; in the patches of sky visible here and there through the foliage, I saw an enormous red-and-white striped hot-air balloon floating past, with a basket hanging down (and a moustachioed fellow waving to everyone from the basket with an orange handkerchief). I saw a blond boy ride by on a bicycle, zigzagging down a path; a man in a long white tunic, with flowing hair and a black beard and moustache, playing the harmonica (this man's eyes recalled the eyes of women, and the calm of certain lakes); a woman who, at almost the extreme left of my field of vision, was moulding clay with her white, slender-fingered hands (and I realised that her beautiful sculpture would never be finished, that she wasn't concerned with giving it a final shape). I watched the constant comings and goings in the greenery, as far as the eye could see, from where I stood in the basement, a few yards beneath the earth's surface; and then, with the key in my pocket, I got to work on the little hole in the wall, making it wider, and I heard the man playing melodies on his harmonica, now further away, and the sound of the sea in the distance, and birdsong, and I heard children shouting, also a long way off, and a woman's laughter; and every time I stopped scraping, overcome by the heat of the basement, covered in sweat, weak with hunger and thirst, I'd bring my eye back to the hole and see the girl with her apple, or a woman, nude and majestic on her white horse, her red hair cascading down her back, and my strength would return and I'd carry on working, and then once again I'd hear the sound of the sea, the creaking of hammocks in the park, the blonde girl's song, and that constant, rhythmic noise that had brought me down to the basement, years before, when this hole in the wall was only a tiny speck. Now the key is worn to a nub and my fingers are covered in blisters and scars, but the hole is still getting bigger. I can fit my fist through it now, the field of vision has widened and I can see the men carding their wool, the swimmers leaping tirelessly off the high rock into the stream, the green-eyed woman waiting on the other bank – and the rays of sunlight shimmering, with golden reflections, through her azure hair.

Tr. KS

THE THINKING-ABOUT-GLADYS MACHINE (NEGATIVE)

Before going to bed I make my daily rounds of the house, to check everything's in order; the window in the small bathroom at the back is closed, and the horse with its throat slit is still rotting in the tub; I shut the door, so the smell doesn't reach my brother-in-law's bedroom; in the kitchen, the tap is off and I turn it on, just enough that it drips; the window is open, letting in the cold night air and the thick climbing plants from the garden; banana skins and tea leaves are still mounting up in and around the rubbish bin; the dregs of some red wine are left in the bottle, and I see flies floating on the surface, dead and alive; the dining-room clock, when I switch on the light, begins to strike twelve and the cuckoo's trapdoor opens and out comes the enormous snake, which slithers interminably down to the floor and then disappears back under the base; on the table, the remains of the feast; wine stains on the tablecloth, along with the fat lady's pink knickers and the still-lit end of the bald Englishman's cigar; the library is in total silence, and the stranger, with his back to me, is reading in the darkness — and at the thought of him a shiver runs down my spine; the high little window that looks onto the air shaft is open, and through it you can hear the roar of the sea and the shouts of night fishermen; the living room is full of people, men and women, lined up side by side, facing the wall with their arms above their heads; I go into the bedroom and find the woman in my bed, naked; she promises to wake me tomorrow at the usual time; I take hundreds of packets of condoms from the nightstand drawer, stuff my pyjama pockets with them, go into the wardrobe and lock the door from the inside.

In the early hours, I wake up shivering. Someone has opened the little window in the wardrobe and I have a fever, I'm drenched in sweat and my left eye hurts. I shout for a doctor or an ambulance, but I'm in the middle of a desolate field and no one can hear my cries.

Tr. AM

TRANSLATOR'S AFTERWORD

The protagonists of these stories – for the most part sol-itary, methodical men who resemble Levrero himself in a hazy, underwater sort of way – can often be found crawling through tunnels. Or peeling back wallpaper, scratching at plaster, rummaging in attics and venturing down to base-ments. They occupy houses that are at once familiar and strange, with padlocked doors, inexplicable noises behind cupboards and intransitable jungles beyond immaculate lawns. Writing, for Levrero, is about exploration, and just as his characters pad up and down their Escher-like hall-ways in pursuit of hidden truths, he roams the recesses of his own mind.

The stories in *The Thinking-About-Gladys Machine* were written between 1966 and 1969, concurrently with Levrero's first novel, *La ciudad* (*The City*). Together, these works mark the beginning of his 'imaginative period', which began when the twenty-six-year-old Levrero decamped from Montevideo to the Uruguayan seaside resort of Piriápolis in the middle of winter following a personal crisis and began to write, feverishly and for the first time in his life. The bizarre, hallucinatory texts he produced during this period won him an early cult following in Uruguay and Argentina, and remain the favourites of many Levrero aficionados to this day. His later, autobiographical works, such as *Empty Words* (first published in Spanish in 1996) and *The Luminous Novel* (published posthumously in 2005), find him looking wistfully back on this creative frenzy, longing for his imagination to take flight in the same way once more.

The imagination, for Levrero, is less literary tool than spiritual portal: 'the doorway, the means of communicating with deep-down things that are hidden from the consciousness'. He was, in the words of his ex-student Gabriela Onetto, 'totally committed to his soul, to the exploration of his being on all possible planes' – including dreams, visions, intuitions, symbolic images and other manifestations of the unconscious, which he saw as the 'essential raw material of art'. Writing is at once the means by which he investigates and the unfurling product of these investigations; pen in hand, he moves through his inner world with a caretaker's unflappable diligence, peering behind furniture and underneath floorboards in search of mysteries that lie just out of sight.

'When the author knows too much about the plot,' Levrero said, 'he ends up in a hurry to tell it, and literature falls by the wayside.' His own stories, meanwhile, often begin as puzzles posed by his unconscious, as he explained in a 1992 'imaginary interview' he conducted with himself:

I notice that something is bothering me: an image, a series of words, or simply a mood, an atmosphere, an environment. The clearest example would be an image or mood from a dream, after waking up in the morning; sometimes you spend a long time almost tangled up in that dream-fragment [. . .] When this goes on for several days, I take it as a sign that there's something there I need to deal with, and the way to deal with it is to recreate it.

As such, imagination is very different to invention, which Levrero scorned as simply making things up. 'I'm talking about things I've experienced', he maintained, 'but generally I haven't experienced them on the plane of reality that biographies tend to make use of.' The stories in this collection – stories in which trained spiders perform acrobatics in rented rooms, tiny women pour out of the bathroom taps, and armies of gardeners tug gently at blades of grass to make them grow – are, in a sense, autobiographical too.

One thing that makes Levrero's imaginative project so unusual is that, though deeply personal, it's never insular. He is a generous host within his inner world, an explorer but also a guide. No matter where he goes, be it through his wardrobe mirror and out the other side, or into the labyrinthine workings of his own cigarette lighter, he always takes the reader with him. Much of this is down to his unmistakeable voice: Levrero is an affable, companionable narrator, inquisitive yet unfazed, with an earnest desire to make himself understood and an eye for absurd comic detail. When one protagonist hears a mysterious noise somewhere in his house, he carefully specifies that it sounds like 'a ping-pong ball, a bit larger than the typical kind, bouncing rhythmically [. . .] or a wooden hammer, wrapped in cloth, knocking on a thick iron pipe'; when another opens a cupboard and a corpse lands on top of him, he has the presence of mind to wonder if it reminds him of his cousin Alfredo.

Recognising a person in their writing voice, Levrero has said, is like recognising a person in a dream: you know on some profound, intangible level that it's them, even if there's no external resemblance. In this way, Levrero is present in every sentence he writes. Though the stories in this collection are some of his earliest work and show him experimenting with various modes and styles, from the B-movie-esque dystopia of 'Jelly' to the Lewis Carroll-influenced adventure of 'The Basement', via the syntactically preposterous comic tour de force that is 'The Boarding House', the prose is always instantly recognisable as his. This is what makes translating him such an immense, through-the-looking-glass pleasure: once you feel his voice begin to take shape, it's so beguiling and distinctive that it solves your translation dilemmas for you. There may be many ways of phrasing something in English, but only one sounds like exactly what Levrero would say.

It is an immense pleasure, too, to think of these stories being read in translation. Levrero, once a cult figure whose books changed hands like contraband, is now recognised as one of the most inventive and idiosyncratic figures of twentieth-century Latin American letters, and this English *Gladys* will, I hope, invite many new readers into his universe.

Annie McDermott
Hastings, May 2024

MARIO LEVRERO, REALIST

TRANSLATOR'S NOTE

It may be surprising to discover that Mario Levrero — whose early works have drawn justifiable comparison to Hieronymus Bosch and M.C. Escher — considered himself a realist. Generally viewed as an author of fantastic literature and even of sci-fi, Levrero made a point of pushing back against these categorisations in interviews throughout his career. Judging the case by common sense alone, it would seem the critics got it right: *The Thinking-About-Gladys Machine* seems like realism's polar opposite. When it comes to Levrero, however, common sense is rarely a friend. So let's take his claim seriously and ask: what did Mario Levrero mean by realism?

For Levrero, the scene generally referred to as the 'real world' is stifling, and, worse yet, boring. Awfully. It's full of overcrowded boarding houses and unhelpful family members. Day after day, grating rituals of routine and submission call us to the same desk at the same hour. We find the majority of the characters in *The Thinking-About-Gladys Machine* in such settings. Exhausted, alienated, and unsure what to do about it, they suffer from too much of

163

this so-called 'reality,' penned up in domestic spaces so stultifying they seem like characters themselves. Thankfully for us, that's not where Levrero ends his stories; instead, that's precisely where he has them begin.

A believer in (and deep-diver into) the Freudian unconscious, Levrero claims to source his images there, where society and the individual meet head-on. It's a site where proto-linguistic nightmares bubble up and sweet images flow freely, where the full weight of the world and spiritual liberation entwine. 'According to Freud,' Levrero notes, 'all antinomies exist together in the unconscious.'[1] That he should underscore this schismatic aspect of psychoanalytical thought feels important given the personalities of Levrero's characters, whose dissatisfactions become the very wellsprings of their creative impulses, and even their joys.

Not only does Levrero claim that his nearly surrealist tales are realism, he also claims that much of what culture deems perfectly normal is, in fact, stuff of the fantastic. And here is where Levrero's ideas show their fangs, and his deceptively dreamy writings become quite radical, even counter-cultural. He asks: 'Is a man who wakes up at seven a.m., puts on a suit and tie, and goes to work for someone else *not* fantastical (however usual)? Is it not fantastical, in fact, that this situation is *not* widely seen as unusual?'[2] With two brief

---

1   Carlos María Domínguez. 'Levrero para armar,' *Brecha*, May 12, 1989.
2   Hugo J. Verani. 'Conversación con Mario Levrero,' *Nuevo texto crítico*, Vol. VIII, No. 16/17, June 1996.

questions, which turn this upstanding member of society into an uncanny emblem of the unimaginative regime, Levrero breaks the illusion of naturalness through which the 'real world' asserts its unquestioned authority. Through the cracks seeps a desire for new, freer behaviours and arrangements.

Take the narrator of 'The Golden Reflections,' for instance, a dead ringer for the businessman described above. The story opens with him dutifully checking his appearance in the mirror before work, to which he has never arrived late, and where he is an ideal employee, even if he doesn't always agree with his boss. His entire life gets thrown off course when he begins to fixate on the source of a mysterious knocking sound somewhere in his house. Having pursued it from room to room, he ends up in his basement, where the noise leads him to a tiny hole in the wall, through which a needle-thin beam of light shines. Peering through this de facto peephole, he glimpses a delightful scene straight out of Botticelli (or Botticelli touched up by Renoir and Magritte): hot air balloons flown by mustachioed gentlemen, children at play, and nude women on horseback, all drifting freely about of a beautiful afternoon in a lush bit of nature. With a key, he scratches at the hole, slowly widening his vantage point. In the end, we are surprised to find that years have passed, yet there he remains, scraping doggedly at the hole – his key a stub and his fingers covered in blisters and scars – awaiting the moment when it will be large enough for him to slip through and escape.

Now, did this man throw his life away? (Did Carlitos, as well, in his life-long pursuit to discover what was in his basement? Or the man in his bedroom who crawled through a dismantled lighter into an another world?) Some may say so. At the very least, his boss probably wasn't thrilled. But it could also be argued that he found a truer one, one fuelled by his own innate curiosity, excitement, and that which his previous life lacked most: hope. There is something profoundly liberatory about this re-evaluation, which inverts societal norms and suggests that our most peculiar intuitions may be, in fact, the seat of our reality. For Levrero, this reality was to be searched out, eyes against the peephole, viewing the stuff of the unconscious in all its inaccessible, provocative glory. And that's just what he did.

Kit Schluter

Dear readers,

As a publisher of shamelessly literary books, in addition to bookshop sales, we rely on subscriptions from people like you in order to publish in line with our values.

All of our subscribers:

- receive a first edition copy of each of the books they subscribe to
- are thanked by name at the end of our subscriber-supported books

BECOME A SUBSCRIBER,
OR GIVE A SUBSCRIPTION TO A FRIEND

Visit andotherstories.org/subscribe to help make our books happen. You can subscribe to a selection of the books we're in the process of making. To purchase books we have already published, we urge you to support your local or favourite bookshop and order directly from them – the often unsung heroes of publishing.

OTHER WAYS TO GET INVOLVED

If you'd like to know about our upcoming books and events, please follow us via:

- our monthly newsletter, sign up here: andotherstories.org
- Facebook: facebook.com/AndOtherStoriesBooks
- Instagram: @andotherpics
- TikTok: @andotherbooktok
- X: @andothertweets
- Our blog: andotherstories.org/ampersand

OUR SERIES DESIGN

The inside text is set in Albertan Pro and Linotype Syntax. Albertan was created by Jim Rimmer in 1982. It was originally made for use in hand-setting limited edition books at Jim Rimmer's own Pie Tree Press. Syntax was created by Hans Eduard Meier in 1968.

Our jacket design is by Elisa von Randow, Alles Blau Studio, who said: 'Choosing simplicity and bringing the author's work to the cover was the starting point suggested by the editors. The next step was to choose a typeface that would convey the contemporary and bold spirit of the publisher's catalogue. After many studies, the simplest and most radical idea was chosen.' The jacket's typeface is Stellage, designed by Mark Niemeijer and released in 2020 by SM Foundry.

OUR MATERIALS

And Other Stories books are printed and bound in the UK using FSC-certified paper from the most ecological paper mills, stamped with a biodegradable foil. In a North of England collaboration, our jacket's card stock is Vanguard, a paper manufactured by James Cropper. Nestled among the Lake District fells, papermaking craftsmanship and steward-ship of the natural environment are integral to all operations at the James Cropper mill. As a specialist in upcycling fibre, James Cropper created the world's first recycling process dedicated to upcycling takeaway coffee cups into fine papers. The cover fibres of the book you're reading had a previous life holding espresso.

The
Luminous
Novel

Mario Levrero

Translated by Annie McDermott

WINNER
ENGLISH PEN
AWARD

THE LUMINOUS NOVEL

A writer attempts to complete the novel for which he has been awarded a big fat Guggenheim grant, though for a long time he succeeds mainly in procrastinating – getting an electrician to rewire his living room so he can reposition his computer, buying an armchair, or rather, two: 'In one, you can't possibly read: it's uncomfortable and your back ends up crooked and sore. In the other, you can't possibly relax: the hard backrest means you have to sit up straight and pay attention, which makes it ideal if you want to read.'

Insomniacs, romantics and anyone who's ever written (or failed to write) will fall in love with this compelling master-piece told by a true original, with all his infuriating faults, charming wit and intriguing musings.

'*The Luminous Novel* could qualify as a new instalment in the literature of boredom, except that it's too charmingly, haplessly funny to be boring.'

LILY MEYER, *NPR*

'Levrero's greatest work, which he wrote by forcing himself to write it, knowing beforehand that what he wanted to write was impossible.'

ALEJANDRO ZAMBRA

'Never has a book about the process of writing a novel – or in fact avoiding writing a novel – been so compelling and accurately rendered. Mario Levrero turns the act of procrastination into a supreme art form.'

BENJAMIN MYERS

Translated by Annie McDermott

Empty Words

MARIO LEVRERO.

'One of the funniest and most influential writers of recent times. This book might change your life, or at least your handwriting.' ALEJANDRO ZAMBRA

EMPTY WORDS

An eccentric novelist decides to go back to basics on his journey of self-improvement: he will strip out the literary aspect of his writing and simply improve his handwriting. The novelist begins to keep a notebook of handwriting exercises, hoping that if he is able to improve his penmanship, his personal character will also improve. What begins as a mere physical exercise becomes involuntarily coloured by humorous reflections and tender anecdotes about living, writing, and the sense – and nonsense – of existence.

The first book by Mario Levrero to be translated into English, *Empty Words* is the perfect introduction to a major author and a significant point of reference in Latin American writing today.

'One of the funniest and most influential
writers of recent times. This book might change
your life, or at least your handwriting.'
ALEJANDRO ZAMBRA

'An eccentric, funny, and original novel: philosophical
but playful, short but obsessive, ironic but
desperate, and theoretical but intimate.'
DANA SPIOTTA